The Mystery of
the Missing Mascot

Nancy was almost halfway to the custodian's office when she felt an odd sensation—the hairs along the back of her neck were prickling. She whirled around. Behind her the hallway was empty.

It's your imagination, she told herself as she started toward the office again.

Then she gasped as a gloved hand grabbed her roughly from behind. It clamped down across her mouth. Another hand covered her eyes.

Though Nancy struggled furiously, she felt herself being pushed down the hall. She heard a door opening, and then she was shoved hard.

Nancy fell to the floor. The last sliver of light disappeared as the door slammed shut. She was alone, trapped in a small, pitch-black space.

On the other side of the door, a key turned, locking her in.

Nancy Drew
Mystery Stories

Available from MINSTREL Books

119

NANCY DREW®

THE MYSTERY OF THE MISSING MASCOT

CAROLYN KEENE

A MINSTREL® BOOK

PUBLISHED BY POCKET BOOKS

New York   London   Toronto   Sydney   Tokyo   Singapore

This book is a work of fiction. Names, characters, places, and incidents are products of the author's imagination or are used fictitiously. Any resemblance to actual events or locales or persons, living or dead, is entirely coincidental.

A MINSTREL PAPERBACK *Original*

A Minstrel Book published by
POCKET BOOKS, a division of Simon & Schuster Inc.
1230 Avenue of the Americas, New York, NY 10020

Copyright © 1994 by Simon & Schuster Inc.
Produced by Mega-Books of New York Inc.

All rights reserved, including the right to reproduce
this book or portions thereof in any form whatsoever.
For information address Pocket Books, 1230 Avenue
of the Americas, New York, NY 10020

ISBN: 0-671-87202-8

First Minstrel Books printing July 1994

10 9 8 7 6 5 4 3 2 1

NANCY DREW, NANCY DREW MYSTERY STORIES,
A MINSTREL BOOK and colophon are registered trademarks
of Simon & Schuster Inc.

Cover art by Aleta Jenks

Printed in the U.S.A.

Contents

1

An Ominous Message

"Can you believe River Heights is so excited about a high school softball game?" Nancy Drew asked as she and her friend Bess Marvin walked down Main Street toward Vida's Sandwich Shop.

Although it was a quiet Sunday morning and most of the shops were closed, nearly every storefront displayed the bright blue and white colors of River Heights High. The sports shop window was filled with blue and white sweatshirts, and Cody's Cameras displayed a poster-size photo of the girls' softball team. Many of the other stores had signs cheering on the River Heights Wildcats to beat Red Rocks High.

Bess pushed back the visor of the blue River Heights baseball cap she was wearing. "Check out the bakery," she said in amazement.

The bakery window displayed a large rectangular cake with blue and white icing. Bess read aloud the message: "Congratulations, River Heights, Eastern Conference Champions!"

She turned to Nancy with a worried glance. "Don't you think they ought to wait until we actually win before baking a cake like that? Today is only the play-off game."

Nancy pushed back a windblown strand of her reddish blond hair. "It does seem a little premature when we've still got two games to go. Then again, this is the first time in years River Heights has made it to the play-offs. And against Red Rocks—our archrival!" She glanced at her watch as they reached Vida's Sandwich Shop. "It's eleven-thirty now, and the game starts at two. Do you think we'll have time to search for a birthday present for Hannah before then?"

Hannah Gruen, the Drews' housekeeper, had lived with Nancy and her father ever since Nancy's mother died when Nancy was very young. Over the years she'd become family to the Drews.

"No problem," Bess said. "First food, then shopping—that's what I consider a perfect agenda."

The two girls went into the sandwich shop and settled themselves in a booth near the back. Nancy ordered a salad, and Bess ordered soup and a sandwich. As the waitress left with their order, two teenage girls sat down at the counter.

2

"They both play on the softball team," Bess whispered to Nancy. "I recognize them from when George was on the team."

George Fayne was Bess's first cousin. The two cousins were almost complete opposites— George lived for sports, Bess for clothing, food, and boys. Both were Nancy's best friends, however, and like Nancy, they had graduated from River Heights High the year before.

"Isn't that Tyra Walker?" Nancy asked, nodding toward the taller girl, who had short black hair and light brown skin. "I think I remember her from last year's school play."

"That's right," Bess said. "And sitting next to her is Louisa Esposito, the team pitcher. She's supposed to be amazing. I've never seen her play, but her pitches have been clocked at something like thirty-five miles an hour. Last year George kept saying that they ought to take Louisa off the junior varsity team and put her on varsity."

"Why didn't they?" Nancy asked as she studied the small-boned girl with long, curly dark hair.

"She was only a sophomore then," Bess explained. "And you know Coach Marks. She feels the varsity teams ought to be chosen from the upper grades." Bess frowned, concentrating. "I think I heard from someone that Louisa and Coach Marks have had a few run-ins."

Nancy winced. "Is Coach Marks laying down

3

the law again?" Coach Marks was famous for being strict with her athletes, particularly anyone who had an ego. "The team is what matters. We have no stars here," was her favorite saying.

Bess shrugged. "I'm not sure what's going on. George has been away at that tennis clinic, so I haven't been getting all the sports gossip."

"Why don't we go wish them luck?" Nancy suggested.

The two friends went up to the counter, where Tyra and Louisa were studying the menu.

"Hi," Bess said. "Tyra, Louisa, this is my friend Nancy Drew. We just wanted to wish you luck before the game."

Tyra smiled at Nancy. "Aren't you the one who solves all those mysteries?"

"I try," Nancy said. Nancy was, in fact, a well-known amateur detective. But that day she was more interested in talking about the upcoming game. "How's it going?" she asked. "You two must be psyched for the game."

Tyra nodded and Louisa stared at the menu.

That's odd, Nancy thought. Neither one of the girls had that pregame excitement she'd seen so often in George. "Is Red Rocks really as tough as everyone says?" she asked.

Neither of the girls answered. Instead, they exchanged a troubled glance.

"Is something wrong?" Nancy asked, her curiosity aroused.

4

Louisa gave a hollow laugh. "You could say that."

"What is it?" Bess asked. "Is there something we can do to help?"

"No one can help," Louisa answered. "I'm off the team. Off the team and out of the game."

"You can't be," Bess said indignantly. "You're the reason River Heights finally made it to the play-offs."

"That's not true," Louisa said at once. "There are a lot of strong players this year."

"Why were you cut?" Nancy asked.

"I missed three practices," Louisa said bitterly. "My mother works nights, and my younger brother's been sick. During Thursday's practice I had to take care of him. It was my third no-show. So on Friday Coach Marks gave me the ax."

"I'm sure the coach would understand—" Nancy began.

Tyra shook her head. "Coach Marks has an unbreakable rule: Miss three practices and you're out—no excuses, no exceptions."

"How could she cut the pitcher two days before the big play-off game?" Bess demanded in an outraged tone.

Louisa shrugged and stood up. "Ask the coach." She turned to Tyra. "I guess I'm not hungry after all. I'll see you later. Play a good game, okay?"

"Yeah," Tyra said in a dejected voice.

5

Nancy saw the waitress bringing out the food she and Bess had ordered. "Do you want to join us at our booth?" she asked Tyra.

"No, thanks," Tyra said. "I guess I'm not that hungry either. I think I'm going to go over to the school and warm up."

"Good luck," Nancy said.

Tyra gave her a sad smile. "With Louisa out, we're going to need more than luck."

As Tyra left the sandwich shop, Nancy and Bess returned to their booth. Bess helped herself to a slice of the hot bread that was served with her soup. "Red Rocks High has beaten our softball team every year for the last ten years," she said. "I was sure this would be our big breakthrough."

Nancy glanced up at the blue and white crepe paper strung from the restaurant's ceiling. "So was everyone else in River Heights. But remember, Louisa said the whole team was strong." Bess still looked downcast, and Nancy decided to change the subject. "I need your help," she said. "Hannah's birthday is on Friday, and I don't know what to get her."

Bess's blue eyes twinkled. "You've come to the right person—shopping problems are my specialty. How about some jewelry or a nice wool sweater?"

"I've gotten her those for other birthdays. You know," Nancy said thoughtfully, "Hannah loves to go to art museums and galleries. Maybe I could find her a piece of art—a print or a sketch."

"Let's try the Thompson Art Galley," Bess suggested. "It's in that wonderful old Victorian house—I love going there. Besides, Maggie Thompson's got great taste. Just about everything in there is gorgeous."

"Sounds like the place to start," Nancy agreed.

After they'd finished eating and paid the check, the two girls got into Nancy's blue Mustang and set off. Nancy drove along a winding tree-lined road that led out of the center of town. The Thompson Gallery soon came into view, a big white wooden house, with a wide wrap-around veranda and gingerbread trim edging the roof. Maggie Thompson had inherited it from her grandfather and converted it into a spacious gallery.

Nancy pulled into the parking lot at the back of the building, then the two friends walked around to the entrance and opened the tall door that led into the entry hall.

Maggie Thompson, a slender woman with long, silver-gray hair that fell halfway down her back, was sitting at the oak reception desk at the end of the hallway. "Nancy, Bess, what a pleasant surprise!" she said. Maggie, a longtime friend of Nancy's father, Carson Drew, had known Nancy and her friends for years. According to Mr. Drew, Maggie had once been a painter herself.

"Please have a look around," she told the girls. "I've got lots of wonderful new pieces."

Nancy and Bess began to wander through the ground floor of the old house. The room that had once been the kitchen was hung with still lifes, painted in deep fall colors. The drawing room featured a series of landscapes.

Nancy and Bess made their way into the high-ceilinged dining room that served as the main gallery. A stack of large canvases leaned against a wall. Only one painting was hung, a riveting portrait of a young man sitting on the edge of a cliff, staring across a wooded mountain valley.

"He's gorgeous!" Bess said.

"Yes, he is," Maggie agreed, coming up behind them. "That's one of Burt Horenstein's. It was painted two years ago."

Nancy looked at the painting with new interest. "Isn't Horenstein the artist who just died?"

"That's right," Maggie said. "Horenstein is River Heights's most famous artist—he graduated from River Heights Art Academy about twenty-five years ago. Did either of you ever meet him?"

Both Nancy and Bess shook their heads.

"Here, I'll show you some photographs," the gallery owner offered. She led the two girls into the study, where she took a leather-bound photo album from a shelf. "This was Horenstein at his last show," she said, pointing to a picture of a lean, bearded man wearing thick glasses. "And this"—she turned to another photo—"was Horenstein with some of the other students from the academy. He was about nineteen then."

"Did he go to River Heights High before the academy?" Bess asked curiously.

"No," Maggie answered. "The Horensteins moved to River Heights the year that Burt entered the academy."

"What an outfit!" Bess giggled, pointing to the shabby tuxedo jacket that Horenstein wore over paint-splattered overalls.

Maggie gave a soft laugh. "Burt never cared about clothing. And when he was in the academy, he was your typical penniless artist. He might have been the most talented student there, but he didn't really begin to sell his work until about five years after he got out of school."

"I bet his work is worth a fortune now," Nancy said.

"Absolutely," Maggie said. "Art always becomes more valuable when the artist dies. Since Burt's death, the prices on his paintings have skyrocketed. He'd be amazed if he knew what his paintings sell for now."

Nancy sighed. "I guess I won't be buying Hannah a Horenstein. I sure would love to see more of them, though."

"You're in luck," Maggie said, closing the photo album. "A week from today we're having a

Horenstein retrospective here at the gallery." She pointed to the stack of canvases leaning against the wall. "We'll have pieces spanning his entire career. You should both come to the opening."

"I'll definitely be there," Nancy promised. "But right now I'm looking for a birthday present for Hannah."

Maggie looked thoughtful. "I might have just the thing, but not until tomorrow. We're getting in a shipment of small paintings, mostly still lifes—the sort that Hannah loves. Some of them are going to be very reasonably priced."

"That sounds perfect," Nancy said. "I'll stop by sometime tomorrow and check them out."

Nancy glanced at her watch as she and Bess left the gallery. "We still have some time before the softball game. Why don't we go back to my house and grab some snacks?"

"A seriously excellent idea," Bess agreed, getting into Nancy's blue sports car.

A short time later Nancy and Bess reached the Drew house. "It's awfully quiet here," Bess said as they went inside. "Where are your dad and Hannah?"

"Hannah's visiting a friend, and Dad's at work," Nancy said.

"Your dad's working on a Sunday?"

"He's preparing a case that goes to trial tomorrow." Nancy's father, Carson Drew, was a well-known criminal lawyer. "Why don't you see what's in the fridge?" Nancy suggested. "I'll just check the answering machine."

Seeing the message light flashing on the machine, Nancy pressed the Play button and waited as the tape rewound.

"I found some apples and some chips—" Bess started to say as she came in from the kitchen. She stopped as they both heard a familiar voice.

"Nancy, this is Dr. Ryan at River Heights High," the message began.

"As in Principal Loretta Ryan?" Bess asked in disbelief. "Why would she call—"

"I'm sorry to bother you at home on a Sunday," the principal went on in an agitated tone. "But I'd appreciate it if you could come over to the high school as soon as possible. I don't quite know how to describe it—I don't actually know how it happened—but a serious crime has been committed at River Heights High!"

2

The Cupboard Was Bare

Nancy played the high school principal's message a second time, just to make sure she'd gotten it all.

"I've never heard Dr. Ryan sound so upset," Nancy told Bess.

"Dr. Ryan's always so cool," Bess agreed. "Remember when Johnny Westerburgh slipped that iguana onto the podium before one of her speeches, and she just picked it up and asked, 'Has someone misplaced a lizard?'"

Nancy laughed at her friend's perfect mimicry of the principal's controlled voice. "I wonder why she's at school on a Sunday. We'd better get over there and see what the problem is." Although she didn't want there to be any problems at River Heights High, Nancy couldn't deny that she loved the excitement of starting a new case.

Nancy and Bess got back into Nancy's car and headed toward River Heights High.

Twenty minutes later the wide green lawn that fronted the high school came into view. Behind it wide marble stairs led into the old North Wing of the building. Nancy drove to the side of the school, where a narrow tarmac drive led to the parking lot behind the school. At the back of the school was the South Wing, a very modern addition with computers in every room.

Nancy and Bess walked around to the front of the building and up the marble steps. Nancy swung open the heavy wooden double doors, and she and Bess entered the cool, dimly lit entry. They walked through the silent hallways to the main office. Bess gave Nancy a nervous smile. "The last time I was in the principal's office, it was for my freshman prank."

"You and George painted that statue in front of Town Hall," Nancy remembered.

"I thought it was water-soluble paint," Bess said. "It was supposed to wash right off. But the rain came and the statue stayed neon pink. And George and I spent three weekends sanding it off. I've steered clear of Dr. Ryan ever since."

"Don't worry," Nancy said as she knocked on the door of the principal's office, a small private room inside the main office. "Dr. Ryan's probably forgotten all about it."

Dr. Ryan opened the door. The principal was a

13

tall, elegant-looking woman who wore her dark hair swept up in a French twist. She wore a crisp navy suit with matching blue pumps.

"Nancy," the principal said, "thank you for coming so quickly." Then, seeing Bess, she gave the blond-haired girl a skeptical look. "And, Ms. Marvin—have you given up painting statues?"

"Bess helps me out on a lot of my cases," Nancy said quickly.

"Well, you've got another case here if you'd like," Dr. Ryan said. "Let me show you."

Dr. Ryan led Nancy and Bess down a series of corridors in the North Wing until they reached the gymnasium, at the very end of the old building. A glass-enclosed corridor connected it to the South Wing, and a door opened directly from the gym to the parking lot. "I opened the school about two hours ago so the softball team could warm up for today's conference game," the principal began.

Nancy smiled as she took in the familiar scent of the highly polished wooden floor. Like most of the graduates of River Heights High, she'd spent countless hours in this room.

Her smile faded as her eyes took in the large mahogany trophy case at the back of the room. Its glass doors stood open, and its shelves were completely empty.

"What happened?" Nancy asked in amazement. Normally, the trophy case held an assortment of sports trophies as well as two of River Heights High's most treasured possessions—the large papier-mâché cougar's head and jersey worn by the school mascot. Rumor had it that one year the mascot was lost, and the River Heights teams couldn't win a single game.

"That's what I need you to find out," Dr. Ryan said. "When I came down to the gym this afternoon, I found the trophy case empty and the doors as they are now."

Nancy knelt to examine the small metal lock at the bottom of the doors but was careful not to touch it. "It was jimmied open," she said. Her frown deepened. "Has the softball team seen this yet?"

"Yes," the principal answered. "They're in the locker room now, getting final instructions from Coach Marks. As you can imagine, having this happen right before such an important game has upset them. The girls are particularly upset that Dorothy Hunt's portrait is gone."

Nancy knew well who Dorothy Hunt was. In the early 1920s River Heights didn't offer athletics to girls—until one day Dorothy Hunt marched into a school board meeting and said that she wanted to coach girls' teams. She insisted that she could teach girls to play games like softball and field hockey and turn them into winners. Reluctantly, the school board allowed her to form girls' teams.

Dorothy delivered on her promise and River Heights High's girls' athletic program was born. When Hunt retired, the school had commissioned a portrait of her. Dorothy Hunt had become something of a guardian angel for all the young women of River Heights High.

"I can't believe someone stole Dorothy's portrait," Bess said, her face white with shock.

"Not to mention the mascot's head and jersey, and last year's trophies," the principal said. "We took state titles in football, field hockey, and soccer. All three trophies are gone. Everything that was in this cabinet has been cleaned out, and today of all days! You know the superstition about playing without the mascot."

"Maybe that was the point," Nancy said thoughtfully. "None of the stolen objects is worth that much money. Maybe this was done to shake up the softball team before the play-offs."

"That was my theory, too," the principal said grimly. "There's been a rumor going around that on the day of the championship game, Red Rocks High was going to have a nasty surprise for us. I just never expected them to take the rivalry this far."

"Have you talked to their coach?" Nancy asked as the locker-room door opened and a short, muscular woman with short blond hair emerged.

"Not yet," Dr. Ryan answered. "I put a call in

to the Red Rocks office, but no one answered. But I'll try again before we set off for the game."

"You'll be wasting your time," said the blond-haired woman, striding across the gym to join them.

"Hi, Coach Marks," Nancy said at once.

The coach gave her a curt nod. "Nancy, Bess, good to see you both again. How's George?"

"At a tennis clinic," Bess answered.

"She's got a fine serve," the coach said proudly. "We worked hard on that."

"I've asked Nancy to investigate the break-in," Dr. Ryan explained to the coach.

"Why did you say Dr. Ryan would be wasting her time calling Red Rocks High?" Nancy asked.

"Because Red Rocks had nothing to do with this," the coach said firmly.

"Who else would want to upset our team?" Bess asked.

"Someone who was recently cut from the lineup," Coach Marks replied. "Louisa Esposito is the one responsible for this."

"I know Louisa," Bess blurted out. "She would never do something like that!"

"That's a very serious accusation," Dr. Ryan said to the coach. "Do you have proof?"

"I cut Louisa from the team on Friday," Coach Marks replied. "She was seen hanging around the gym earlier today, when she had absolutely no reason to be there. That girl has a bad attitude. She refuses to follow the rules and then gets angry when she is punished."

"None of that is proof that she's the thief," Nancy pointed out.

Coach Marks gave Nancy an irritated look. "I don't have time to argue right now," she said. "I've got a team waiting in the locker room. We have to go over strategy before I get them on the bus." Turning, she left the gym floor.

One of the gymnasium's doors creaked open, and Nancy saw a dark-haired woman police officer enter the gym. "Dr. Ryan, I'm Officer Nomura. You reported a break-in?"

The principal pointed to the trophy case and explained what was missing.

"Hi, Nancy," said the officer with a smile. Nancy often worked closely with the River Heights Police, and she and Nomura had met before.

The police officer took out a fingerprinting kit and began to dust the trophy case and the immediate area for prints. As she waited, Nancy noticed a man in dark green coveralls entering the gym through the door that led from outside. "Who's that?" she asked the principal softly.

Dr. Ryan glanced at him. "Mr. Berger, our new custodian. He often comes in on weekends to clean up for Monday."

Just then Officer Nomura shook her head.

"Whoever is responsible for the break-in knew enough to wear gloves. I don't see a single print. Were any of the doors into the school forced open?"

"None," said the principal. "Mr. Berger, our custodian, and I checked. Whoever did this either had a key or was let in by someone who did."

"Is the key to the gymnasium different from the front entrance key?" the officer asked.

"Yes," the principal said. "And there are also separate keys for each of the two locker rooms. Most of our teachers have keys to the school and to their own homerooms."

"Is Coach Marks the only one to have a key to the gym?" Nancy asked.

"No," Dr. Ryan replied, "I have a key, as does Mr. Li, the boys' gym teacher. And Mr. Berger has keys to all the rooms in the school."

The police officer noted this on the pad she was holding, then said, "Dr. Ryan, I'd like to ask you about the objects that were stolen."

The door to the girls' locker room opened, and a subdued softball team filed out. Silently they crossed the gym and went out the door that led to the parking lot. None of them looked at the empty trophy case.

Nancy watched through the open door as they milled around the yellow school bus waiting to take them to the conference game. "I'd like to talk to some of the members of the softball team before they take off," she told the principal.

"I'll come with you," Bess volunteered.

Dr. Ryan nodded. "Good idea. I'll catch up with you at the game."

As Nancy and Bess emerged from the gym into the bright spring sunlight, they saw the coach talking to a skinny teenage boy with straight, longish red hair. The boy looked agitated.

"What do you mean the head is gone?" the boy asked loudly. "How can I be the mascot if the head is gone?"

"Who is that?" Nancy asked Bess.

Bess shrugged, but the girl who was standing next to her, an outfielder named Cindy Destino, answered. "That's Gordon McTell," she said. "He wears the mascot uniform at the games. He's really into it. This is a major tragedy for him."

"It's all Louisa Esposito's fault," added another player, a girl named Trisha Lewis.

"Why do you say that?" Nancy asked.

"Louisa was really bitter when she got cut," Trisha answered. "She said Marks was ruining her chance to get an athletic scholarship, and she'd do anything to ruin it for Marks. I think she broke into the trophy case to get even."

"No way," said Tyra Walker, coming up to join them. "Louisa would never do something that would affect the whole team like this. Besides, she's not a thief. This is definitely Red Rocks playing their usual tricks."

"Definitely," agreed a fourth girl, whom Nancy recognized as Kit Washuta, another one of the school's top athletes. "The biggest strike against us isn't some missing mascot—it's the fact that Louisa isn't pitching."

"Ladies!" Coach Marks's voice cut through the discussion. "No gossiping, please! Let's board the bus. We have a play-off game to win today!"

"Coach Marks sure is intense," Bess said as she and Nancy watched the team file onto the bus. "Imagine being that set on winning and still cutting one of your best players."

"George said the coach never bent," Nancy remembered. "Either you play by her rules or you don't play at all. Come on," she said to Bess. "Let's drive over to Red Rocks. This is one game I don't want to miss."

Half an hour later Nancy and Bess pulled into the Red Rocks parking lot. "So where do we start looking for the missing mascot?" Bess asked as they got out of the car.

"Good question," Nancy said. "If Dr. Ryan is right, and the mascot was taken by the Red Rocks team, then we ought to check out the place where the team meets—their locker room." She looked at Bess, who was dressed entirely in River

Heights colors. "It might look a little suspicious if you went in there wearing blue and white," Nancy said. "Maybe I should meet you in the bleachers."

"Okay," said Bess. "I'll get us good seats."

The crowds were streaming toward the softball field that lay behind the three sleek modern buildings of Red Rocks High. Nancy set off in the opposite direction, toward the farthest of the three buildings. She'd been to a basketball game at Red Rocks the year before and remembered that the gym was there. She just hoped the door was open.

The door to the building was open, and Nancy found the gym without trouble. The gym itself was about twice the size of River Heights's. There was no sign of the stolen items.

At the end of the gym was a door that said Girls Locker Room. Nancy's sneakers squeaked as she crossed the shiny wood floor to the locker room. She was about halfway across the gym when the locker-room door opened and five girls in Red Rocks softball uniforms came out.

The girls all seemed to see Nancy at the same moment, and four of them turned questioningly to the fifth girl. The fifth girl was tall and muscular and wore her blond hair in a single, long braid. She carried a wooden softball bat.

"Who are you?" the tall girl called out.

Nancy hadn't prepared a story before coming in. What could she tell them?

Before she could answer, the five girls surrounded her. "That's right, don't answer," their leader said angrily. "You don't have to. We *know* why you're here." She swung the baseball bat high overhead. "We've been expecting a spy from River Heights."

3

Bitter Rivals

Nancy ducked quickly as the girl swung the wooden bat toward her. "You're wrong!" she cried out. "I don't even go to River Heights!"

The girl swung again, backing Nancy toward the wall.

"Carla," said one of the other girls in an alarmed voice. "Chill."

Carla glanced at her teammate and dropped the bat, but she continued to advance on Nancy.

"I'm a reporter with the *River Heights Morning Record*," Nancy invented quickly. "I was hoping to interview the captain of your team."

"I'm Carla Richmond, and I'm the team captain," Carla said, still in a belligerent tone.

"Good," Nancy said. "Now, I'd like to know why you think River Heights would send a spy into your gym."

"Because that's exactly the kind of thing they'd do," said a girl with short brown hair and freckles. "They haven't won a championship in years, and they're desperate for this one."

"You want a story?" asked the girl standing closest to Carla. "I'll tell you what to write. Write that Red Rocks High has never been defeated by River Heights and never will be."

"I can also write about what good sports you all are," Nancy said between her teeth. She didn't like being bullied and was trying not to lose her temper.

At that moment the locker-room door opened and a stocky woman, wearing sweats and a whistle around her neck, looked out. "You five—in here now!" she barked. "The game's about to start."

Nancy watched the five players return to the locker room. She felt relieved that she wasn't going to be out on the field. One thing was for sure—River Heights was in for a rough game.

Nancy left the gym and made her way out to the softball diamond. She spotted Bess on the visitors' side of the bleachers. Next to Bess sat Gordon McTell, glowering down at the field.

Nancy waved and climbed up beside them. Although there were still fifteen minutes till the game began, the stands were nearly full. Nancy could feel the excitement in the air. River Heights had been waiting for years for a chance to make it to the conference play-offs and then advance to the state championship.

Nancy nudged Bess as Dr. Ryan, followed by two other teachers, made her way toward them. "Nancy, Bess, you remember Mr. Calabrese," the principal said, nodding toward the tall, bearded man beside her.

Bess and Nancy nodded and smiled. William Calabrese, River Heights's art teacher, was one of the most popular teachers in the school.

"And this is Ms. Stamos, our new chemistry teacher," Dr. Ryan went on.

Nancy and Bess said hello to the two teachers, and then they all sat down in the stands.

Bess gave Nancy a quick smile. "I wish George were here for this," she said. "She'd love to see River Heights softball in a play-off game." Bess dropped her voice to a whisper. "Did you find anything in the gym?"

"Five very angry Red Rocks players," Nancy answered. "They accused me of being a River Heights spy."

"I still want to know where my costume is," Gordon McTell interrupted. "This is a total disaster! The Red Rocks Rooster will be out there, and River Heights will have nothing. It'll ruin everyone's morale."

"Well, you're wearing a River Heights jacket," Bess suggested. "Why don't you take my hat and go down to the field and dance, anyway?"

26

Gordon shot her a look of withering scorn. "That just shows how much you know about being a mascot. It's the cougar that brings luck, not some guy dancing around in jeans and a jacket. The cougar is the reason we win."

Nancy smiled. "Coach Marks might not agree with you, but I know what you mean. It's a shame this had to happen today."

The first few innings began slowly. Both teams were playing strong defense, and neither could score a run off the other. At that moment River Heights was up with Tyra Walker at bat, and Carla Richmond was pitching to her.

Nancy could see that Tyra was tense. It didn't help that the Red Rocks team was taunting her, Carla Richmond in particular. Carla kept telling Tyra what a sick excuse for a player she was, and it was getting to her. Nancy could see Tyra becoming more rattled with every pitch.

Fortunately, Carla's first two pitches were balls. But the third was a strike, and two other River Heights players had already struck out.

"I'm gonna strike you out!" Carla promised. "Just like the others, you're going down! This is the end, Walker!"

The ball sailed over the plate. Tyra swung wildly, the umpire called a strike, and Carla nearly collapsed laughing on the mound.

"That Carla Richmond! Why don't the referees make her stop?" Bess demanded angrily.

"I don't know," Dr. Ryan said. "But I certainly intend to talk to their principal, Dr. Hollings, about it on Monday."

Nancy didn't mention her encounter in the gym, but privately she was thinking that maybe Dr. Ryan was right—that Red Rocks was behind the break-in. She'd been to all sorts of sports events, both high school and professional, and she'd never seen such a rude team.

Suddenly everyone in the River Heights stands was clapping like mad as Tyra Walker slammed a ball into the outfield. The Red Rocks outfielder missed the catch, and Tyra made it safely to third base. Now River Heights had a chance of scoring. "Tyra! Tyra!" the crowd chanted. Even Gordon McTell had stopped sulking and was on his feet cheering.

Next Trisha Lewis came up to bat. When she hit a grounder toward first, Tyra raced to home plate. Carla Richmond, who was out on the pitching mound, threw the ball home. Only she didn't throw it to her catcher. Instead she sent the ball slamming into Tyra's right leg, even though Tyra had already crossed the plate. Nancy saw the girl grimace in pain.

"Time out!" called one of the referees.

"Did you see that?" Bess asked indignantly. "She deliberately hit Tyra! She's trying to injure her and get her out of the game."

"This wouldn't have happened if the mascot had been out there," Gordon muttered.

"I think it would have," Dr. Ryan said angrily. "I intend to file a written complaint with Dr. Hollings about this Richmond girl."

Nancy watched as Tyra limped back to the bench and Coach Marks wrapped her leg with ice.

"Excuse me," said Mr. Calabrese. "I think I'll take this opportunity to go get a soda."

"I'll come with you," Ms. Stamos offered, smiling at him.

Bess nudged Nancy with her elbow once the two teachers had left. "Do you think they're dating?" she asked in a whisper.

Dr. Ryan fixed Nancy and Bess with a stern stare. "Are you two gossiping about my teachers?"

Nancy gulped and came up with a quick white lie. "Actually, we were just saying how we were surprised to see Mr. Calabrese here. We never thought of him as a sports fan."

"Don't let him fool you," Dr. Ryan said. "Mr. Calabrese has always supported the school sports teams. Ever since he met Dorothy Hunt, that is. She won him over completely."

"He actually knew Dorothy Hunt?" Nancy asked, intrigued.

"He's the one who painted her portrait," the

principal explained. "I believe he was still a student at the art academy when he painted her. Mr. Curry—he was River Heights's principal at the time—had been impressed with Mr. Calabrese when he was in high school. Dorothy was about to retire, so Mr. Curry contacted William and asked if he'd paint her portrait for the school."

"Wasn't that kind of unusual?" Nancy asked. "Commissioning a student to do a portrait?"

Dr. Ryan laughed. "High schools don't have budgets set aside for portraits of their teachers. Mr. Curry wanted to honor Dorothy and did it the most affordable way possible. And though he was only twenty years old, William was quite competent as a portrait artist."

The time-out was soon over and the teams came back onto the field. Nancy watched tensely as River Heights's next batter, Cindy Destino, struck out, and the teams traded places. Tyra Walker was supposed to pitch—she'd pitched the first three innings. But Kit Washuta went to the mound instead, while Tyra sat on the bench. Nancy realized that Tyra must be hurting pretty badly.

A few minutes later Mr. Calabrese returned to the stands, carrying his soda. "What happened to Ms. Stamos?" Bess asked.

Mr. Calabrese nodded toward the crowd at the refreshment stand. "She met a friend from Red

Rocks. I believe they're catching up on the news of someone's wedding."

"What do you mean 'a friend from Red Rocks'?" Gordon demanded.

Mr. Calabrese sighed. "Gordon, just because our schools are athletic rivals doesn't mean that everyone from Red Rocks is the enemy."

"Traitor," Gordon muttered.

"Lighten up," the art teacher muttered back.

"I think I'll get some popcorn," Nancy said. She glanced at Bess, as if to explain that she had to do some more investigating while the Red Rocks team was busy playing. Bess nodded.

"How can you eat at a time like this?" Gordon demanded.

Nancy smiled. "Be back soon."

Nancy made her way down to the edge of the field. She walked toward the food stands and then headed for the Red Rocks gym. This time she knew the locker room would be deserted.

A couple of minutes later, Nancy found herself wandering through the locker room's narrow aisles. A few green metal doors stood ajar—lockers jammed with sweat socks, sneakers, and dark red Red Rocks T-shirts. Gym bags, cotton bandages, and damp towels lay scattered across the benches and floors.

Nancy walked through the room slowly, trying not to disturb anything and yet be as thorough as possible. She peered into the open lockers and beneath the wooden benches. She even checked the shower stalls.

Seeing an open red gym bag on the end of a bench, she glanced at it quickly. Then a familiar shade of blue caught her attention.

Curious, Nancy pulled out a blue River Heights jersey. On the back, instead of a team number, it had a painting of a snarling cougar's head.

It was the mascot's jersey!

Nancy examined the bag carefully. A name had been written on the side with a marker. Though it was now nearly washed out, Nancy could still make out the letters.

They spelled out the name Carla Richmond.

4

Lost and Found

Nancy quickly stuffed the stolen jersey into her own shoulder bag. I've found one of the stolen objects, she thought. Now, where are the others? Does Carla Richmond have them as well? Obviously, the cougar's papier-mâché head wasn't in the gym bag, nor was the portrait of Dorothy Hunt. But what about the missing trophies?

Nancy began to search through the open bag. She pulled out a Red Rocks sweatshirt, a sweatband, and a towel.

The bag still wasn't empty. There was a balled-up T-shirt and maybe something under that. Nancy reached down into the gym bag, then froze. She heard the locker-room door open, followed by the sound of a woman's high heels clicking briskly against the cement floor.

Quickly Nancy replaced the contents of Carla's bag. She couldn't be caught snooping in the Red Rocks locker room!

An attractive woman with short, glossy brown hair came around the row of lockers. "Nancy Drew!" the woman exclaimed. "What a coincidence, meeting you here!"

Nancy forced herself to smile back. She'd been found by Ally Laval, the incredibly nosy reporter for Channel 9, River Heights's local TV station.

Ally leaned back against one of the lockers, looking casually elegant in her tan linen suit. Somehow Ally Laval always was perfectly put together. Nancy remembered seeing her once at the scene of a fire—while everyone else was covered with soot, Ally looked as if she'd just stepped out of a fashion magazine.

"Well, that explains it," Ally said.

"Explains what?" Nancy asked, puzzled.

"Some members of the Red Rocks team told me they found a reporter from the *Morning Record* in the gym before the game," Ally replied. "A friend of mine writes about sports for the *Record,* and I knew she wasn't covering this game. It was you in the gym, wasn't it?"

Nancy ignored the question, determined not to let Ally rattle her. "Maybe you'd like to explain why *you're* here in the locker room when the game is out on the field."

"I don't answer questions—I ask them," the reporter snapped. "You're investigating the break-in at River Heights High, aren't you?"

"No comment," Nancy said evenly.

"Our reporter who covers the police beat told me all about it," Ally went on. She gave Nancy a shrewd look. "Do you think the Red Rocks team is responsible?"

"I don't know," Nancy replied honestly. "I'm still trying to find out." A roar from the softball diamond came in through the open window. "If you'll excuse me," Nancy said, "I'd like to see the rest of the game."

Nancy bought a box of popcorn and made her way back to the stands. The score, she saw, was now tied at six all.

"You missed a great inning," Bess reported. "Kit Washuta and Cindy Destino both hit homers."

Nancy munched on a handful of popcorn. "The locker room wasn't nearly as exciting. I ran into Ally Laval."

"Her again!" Bess said. "Every time we turn around, there's Ally Laval."

"That's how a good reporter is supposed to be," Nancy admitted, "always on the story. I just wish Ally weren't on this one. She knows about the break-in. And I know she's going to make my job harder."

Bess nodded sympathetically, then stood up, applauding as Carla Richmond struck out and the River Heights team came up to bat. Beside Bess, Gordon McTell was on his feet, shouting himself hoarse. "Let's go, River Heights!"

Gordon kept cheering as River Heights's first batter struck out and the second came up to the plate. It was Tyra Walker.

"I wonder if she recovered from that hit she took," Bess said.

Carla Richmond was back on the mound, pitching. She gave Tyra a look that seemed to say she wouldn't mind popping her again.

Nancy winced as a curve ball flew over the plate and Tyra shied away from it.

"Strike one!" the umpire called.

On the mound Carla laughed and wound up for her next pitch. "Get ready for strike two!"

"Go, Tyra!" Gordon screamed. "Don't let Red Rocks psych you out!"

"Strike two!" the umpire called.

"She's lost her nerve," Bess said.

"This is a piece of cake!" Carla Richmond called out. "Strike number three coming up!" She wound up and sent a low underhand pitch across the plate. But this time Tyra's bat connected with a solid crack. The ball went flying out of the diamond, out beyond the stands.

"She did it!" Gordon screamed.

"She certainly did!" Mr. Calabrese agreed as a beaming Tyra took an easy lap around the bases. In the stands all of the River Heights fans were on their feet, cheering. For the second time in the game, River Heights was ahead.

As Trisha Lewis stepped up to bat, Nancy decided it was time to tell the principal what she'd found. "Excuse me, Dr. Ryan," Nancy said, "could I talk with you for a moment?" Nancy nodded toward the ground. "Not up here in the stands."

"I suppose so," the principal said reluctantly, and followed Nancy down to the field.

"I want to show you what I found in the Red Rocks locker room," Nancy said. She reached into her shoulder bag and took out the blue jersey. "Do you recognize this?"

"Of course," Dr. Ryan said. "It's our mascot's jersey. You found *this* in their locker room?"

Nancy nodded. "In Carla Richmond's gym bag."

"What about the other missing objects?"

"I didn't find any of those," Nancy said, "but my search was cut short. Ally Laval came into the locker room. She knows all about the stolen items from the trophy case."

"Wonderful," the principal said with a sigh. "The last thing the school needs is publicity about the break-in." She looked at the mascot's shirt in her hand and then out at the field. "I'm tempted to take this to the referees right now and get Red Rocks disqualified from the conference."

"Are you going to?" Nancy asked.

The principal took a deep breath. "No," she said. "I'm a great believer in 'innocent until proven guilty.' What we have here is evidence, but it's not concrete proof. Besides, I'm not sure how to explain your searching the Red Rocks locker room. They might protest that it was an illegal search and seizure. I'd like you to continue the investigation, though, until we find the rest of the stolen objects."

"I'd be glad to," Nancy said.

The principal smiled at her. "Then let's go back and watch the end of this game."

One hour later Nancy left the stands with a jubilant group of River Heights fans. Their softball team had come through—they'd won the play-off game for the eastern conference. Next week it was on to the conference championship —and if they won that as well, the final game for the state title!

Nancy was just crossing the field when she saw the dejected Red Rocks team heading for the locker room. "I'll be back in a minute," she told Bess. "There's something I have to do."

"Carla," she called out, running up to the Red Rocks team captain. "Could I talk with you?"

"Want to interview a loser?" Carla asked bitterly. "Who are you, anyway? That other reporter, Ally Laval, said the *Record* didn't send anyone to cover the game."

Nancy raised her hands in a gesture of surrender. "All right, no more lies," she said. "I'm not a reporter. I'm a detective and—"

"And I'm a brain surgeon," Carla said sarcastically. She turned her back on Nancy and began striding toward the locker room.

"I'm trying to find out who broke into the River Heights gym and stole the items from the trophy case," Nancy said, trailing after her. "I found the mascot's jersey in your gym bag."

That stopped Carla. She swung around angrily. "What were you doing in my gym bag?"

"It was open," Nancy said. "And our mascot's jersey was lying right on top. Where are the other things that were taken?"

"I don't know," Carla said. "Because I didn't have anything to do with it!"

"The evidence was in your bag," Nancy said.

"I really don't need this today," Carla snarled, her gray eyes hard. "I think you're lying—you're trying to frame me. If you don't leave me alone, I'll report you to school security. You had no right to be in our locker room."

Nancy took a deep breath, knowing Carla was right. "All right," she said, "but I'm going to find out who broke into the River Heights gym. You'd better be telling me the truth."

The tall athlete towered over her. "And you'd better not get in my way again. If you do, I swear you'll regret it."

The next morning Nancy stopped by Bess's house. "Want to join me for the second round of the search for Hannah's present?" she invited.

"Of course," Bess said as she got into the blue Mustang. "I never say no to shopping."

"I'm glad," Nancy said. "Because I need to talk to someone about the case."

"But you've solved it already," Bess said. "It's obvious. Carla Richmond is responsible for the break-in and the theft."

"Is she?" Nancy asked in a troubled tone. "I didn't find any of the other stolen objects."

"Something as big as Dorothy's portrait or the mascot's head would be pretty hard to hide in a locker room," Bess pointed out. "The Red Rocks girls must have hidden them somewhere else."

Nancy turned onto a road lined with flowering dogwood trees. "But when I asked Carla about the jersey, she told me she had nothing to do with it," she said.

"And you believed her?" Bess asked.

"I don't know what to believe," Nancy answered. "Winning that game was important to Red Rocks, and they were definitely trying to psych out River Heights. But according to Dr. Ryan, if they were caught stealing from another

40

school, they'd be thrown out of the athletic conference. I'm not sure they'd risk that. Besides, how would Red Rocks students get in and out of a locked gymnasium? The only lock that was broken was the one on the trophy case."

"Maybe one of them sneaked in on Friday, when school was still open, and hid there all weekend?" Bess suggested.

"No, her parents would probably have noticed she was gone," Nancy said. "And Dr. Ryan would have found whoever it was. She was the one who opened the gym on Sunday afternoon."

Thinking out loud, she went on, "Would a member of the Red Rocks team really do that— hide out all weekend, risk being caught by the principal of River Heights, and possibly not make it back in time for the game?" Nancy shook her head as she pulled into the gallery's parking lot. "It just doesn't make sense."

"You think it's someone from River Heights?" Bess asked.

"I'm not sure what to think," Nancy answered. "I just hope it's not Louisa."

"It isn't," Bess said. "That's the one thing I'm sure about."

The two girls got out of the car and entered the gallery. They found Maggie talking to a young woman in a neon orange dress, who was sitting behind the gallery's long oak reception desk.

Maggie smiled at the two friends. "Nancy and

41

Bess," she said, "I'd like you to meet Didi. She's going to be my new assistant."

Didi nodded at the girls. She was chewing gum and loudly popping it, Nancy noticed with surprise. Didi didn't exactly fit in with the gallery's air of quiet elegance.

"Did those small oil paintings come in?" Nancy asked.

"They're over here," Maggie said, leading the girls to a table in the study. "They're unframed canvases, all by the same artist."

Nancy and Bess began looking through the lovely small oil paintings. Some were still lifes—a vase of flowers, a bowl of fruit, a glass jar on a wooden shelf. Others were outdoor scenes or portraits.

"I like this one of the cat sleeping on the checked blanket," Bess said.

"So do I," Nancy agreed, "but Hannah isn't much of a cat person. I think she'd like either this bowl of lilacs or this one of the meadow."

Bess squinted thoughtfully at the two paintings. "I vote for the lilacs. It's kind of like the vase on your hall table."

"The lilacs it is," Nancy agreed. She took the small oil painting up to the desk.

Didi, who was applying orange nail polish to her long nails, looked up in surprise.

"I'd like to buy this painting," Nancy said.

"Cool," Didi replied. She glanced at what was

obviously a list of instructions that Maggie had given her. "Do you want it framed?"

Nancy said she did, and Didi showed her a selection of frames.

"This one, I think," Nancy said, pointing to a frame edged in gold.

"Cool," Didi said again, setting the painting on the desk. She began writing out the order. "Let's see. With framing and tax, the total will come to—" She reached across the desk to grab a calculator, but her hand accidentally knocked over the open bottle of nail polish. A narrow stream of orange oozed across the painting of the lilacs.

"Oh, no!" Nancy cried. Hannah's present was ruined!

"What happened?" Maggie asked, rushing over. She took in the situation at once and sighed deeply. "Didi, this is not a manicure parlor. What was that nail polish doing there?" She gave Nancy an apologetic glance. "Is this the painting you wanted for Hannah?"

Nancy tried not to sound disappointed. "I guess I'd better pick out something else."

"Not necessarily," Maggie said. "I can probably get the nail polish off without hurting the painting."

"You think you can save the picture?" Bess asked doubtfully.

"Pretty sure," Maggie said. "But it may take

me a couple of days—I'm so busy getting ready for the Horenstein show. But it will take a few days anyway for the frame to come in."

"I just need to have it by Friday, for Hannah's birthday," Nancy said.

"I'll call you if there's a problem," Maggie promised.

Once Bess and Nancy stepped outside the gallery, they exchanged a smile. "I wonder how long Didi will last at that job," Nancy said.

Bess laughed. "Maggie's a patient lady, but I have a feeling that either Didi or her nail polish will have to go."

The two girls got back in the car, stopped for gas, then returned to Nancy's house. "So," Bess said as they entered, "since you don't think you've solved the mystery of the missing mascot, what's your next move?"

"I was just wondering the same thing," Nancy said. She stepped into the hallway and found the message light on the answering machine blinking. "Maybe this will give me some clue to follow," she said, pressing the Play button.

"Nancy, it's Dr. Ryan again," the message began. "I believe your case is closed. This morning when Mr. Berger, the custodian, arrived at the school, he found the trophies, the portrait, and the cougar's head—right back in the display case, as if they'd never been gone."

44

5

It's Not Over Yet

"That's an extremely strange message," Bess said as Nancy's answering machine clicked off.

"I'll say," Nancy agreed. "Sometime this past weekend, someone got into the locked gym and stole everything in the trophy case. And now this morning, everything's back."

"Do you think the thief had a change of heart?" Bess suggested.

"Maybe," Nancy said doubtfully. "Or maybe there was something in that display case that he—or she—needed and now doesn't need anymore."

Bess sank down thoughtfully on the arm of a sofa. "What you said before, about the thief no longer needing the stuff? That makes perfect sense if the thief took the mascot just to freak out the team before the game. And it pretty much rules out Lousia—she'd never hurt the team like that."

"Then we're back to Red Rocks being responsible," Nancy said.

"Exactly," Bess agreed. "And since Carla knows you found the jersey in her bag, they probably decided to return everything so that they won't get in trouble."

Nancy ran a hand through her reddish blond hair. "Dr. Ryan said that the returned objects were found by the custodian, Mr. Berger. He was there on Sunday, too. Maybe I should talk to him."

"Why?" Bess asked.

Nancy chewed her lip thoughtfully. "Because I think Dr. Ryan is wrong. This case is far from being closed."

After driving Bess home, Nancy headed back to River Heights High. The first lunch bell was just ringing as she entered the North Wing. The old building's high ceilings made the halls echo as classroom doors slammed open and students poured into the corridors. Nancy smiled as she remembered how eagerly she used to await the lunch bell, as if it were a promise of freedom. It sure wasn't because the cafeteria food was any good.

"Hey, Drew! What are you doing back here?"

46

called out a good-looking senior named Steve Jackson. Steve had had a crush on her the year before. "Did you come to visit me?" he teased.

"Actually, I came to visit Dr. Ryan," Nancy said as she turned toward the principal's office.

"Heartbreaker!"

"You'll survive," Nancy joked back. "Anyway, I heard you were going out with someone."

"Louisa Esposito," Steve told her, smiling. "She's pretty great."

"So I've heard," Nancy said. She liked Steve and she was glad to hear that he was going out with Louisa. It confirmed her good opinion of the girl. "See you later," Nancy said as she reached the office.

"Count on it," Steve told her with a grin.

Nancy knocked on the door of Dr. Ryan's office.

"Come in!" the principal called. She looked up from a desk covered with papers. "Nancy," she said, sounding surprised. "Didn't you get my message?"

"That's why I'm here," Nancy said. "I think the return of the stolen objects is every bit as mysterious as their disappearance. The case doesn't seem closed to me."

"I know what you mean," the principal said. "The puzzle isn't solved. But the problem—that important objects were taken from the school— has been resolved."

"That just makes it more of a mystery," Nancy persisted.

The principal nodded. "It does, but I'm afraid that's not reason enough to pursue the case."

"What do you mean?" Nancy asked.

Dr. Ryan gestured toward the mass of papers on her desk. "Well, the end of the school year is fast approaching, and I have a great deal to do before graduation. I owe reports to the board of education and the superintendent of schools. I'm afraid I don't have time to put together pieces of a puzzle. The important thing is that the stolen objects were returned unharmed."

Nancy nodded. "I understand. But would you mind if I kept working on the case?"

The principal looked reluctant. "The person who stole the objects returned them in perfect condition," she said. "I'd like to believe that whoever is responsible realized it was wrong to steal them. Maybe it was just a prank of some sort. I'm willing to let bygones be bygones."

Nancy sighed in frustration. "It's not that I want to see anyone get in trouble," she said. "But if someone broke into the trophy case once—and got into the locked gym twice—then something similar could happen again. For the safety of the students, we have to solve this."

Dr. Ryan sat back in her chair, a look of surrender on her face. "You always were persuasive, Nancy. Very well, continue the investigation. But please do it quietly. I don't want to draw a lot of attention to this matter."

"Thanks," Nancy said. "I'll try to solve it quickly. But I do need to talk to the people who have keys to the gym—the two gym teachers and Mr. Berger."

"Well, Jack Li, the boys' gym teacher, is in Seattle," the principal said. "A member of his family is ill, and he flew out last Monday."

Nancy perked up. "Would the substitute who's taking his classes for him have the keys?" Nancy asked.

"We don't give out keys to substitute teachers," the principal answered. "Mr. Berger opens the gym for him whenever he needs it."

"Well, then maybe I'll start with Mr. Berger," Nancy said.

"Good luck," the principal told her.

Nancy took the stairs down to the basement of the North Wing. It was quiet down there, quieter than any other part of the school, and its warm, slightly musty smell raised memories for her.

She remembered the first time she'd come down there, for her freshman prank. She had decided to sneak into the basement to the master light controls and shut off the lights in the auditorium during a school assembly. Fortunately, she hadn't been caught, and no students had been harmed by the brief spell of darkness.

As Nancy moved down the hallway, she noticed that the door to the custodian's office was open. The office was exactly as Nancy remembered it—a dimly lit, cramped room, filled with assorted tools and filing cabinets. A tall grayhaired man in dark green coveralls sat with his feet up on the desk. "You looking for something?" he asked.

"Mr. Berger?" Nancy said. She thought she recognized him from the brief glimpse she'd had of him Sunday morning in the gym.

"That's me," the man drawled.

Nancy introduced herself and explained that she was investigating the break-in. "Do you know who locked up the building on Friday afternoon?"

"I did," he replied. "I was the last one in the building."

"And did you lock the gym before you left?"

"I did," Berger snapped. "I lock everything up. What is this—Twenty Questions?"

"Dr. Ryan asked me to investigate," Nancy repeated calmly. "And I—"

"I know who you are, and I don't have anything to say to you," the man broke in rudely. "I already talked to that policewoman. Why should I talk to a kid who thinks she's a detective? Besides, the stuff's all back where it ought to be. Why can't you just leave me alone?"

"Just one question," Nancy said, ignoring his outburst. "When you locked up on Friday afternoon, how do you know that someone wasn't hiding in the gym or in one of the locker rooms?"

"Because I'm responsible for cleaning them," the janitor answered. "I'm telling you—no one was hiding anywhere near the gym."

"That means someone with a key got in sometime after you left on Friday and before Dr. Ryan opened the gym on Sunday," Nancy said, thinking aloud. "And then that person got in again sometime between yesterday afternoon and this morning. Did you lock up yesterday?"

Berger nodded, his eyes narrowed with annoyance. "And I unlocked the school and the gym this morning."

"And you didn't see anything?"

"I saw all the stuff was back in the trophy case," the custodian snapped. "Listen, I'm paid to clean the building and keep its systems running. I'm not a security guard."

Obviously, Nancy thought.

Berger stood up and walked to the door of the cramped office. "I've got work to do." He held the door open, obviously wanting her to go. Nancy left the custodian's office without another word.

But as she headed toward the stairs, Berger's voice called after her. "You be careful now, Miss Drew," he said. "Being nosy can get you in big trouble."

Was that supposed to be a threat? Nancy

wondered. Or was Berger just a cranky man who didn't like people asking questions?

Either way, there was no point in staying in the basement. Nancy glanced at her watch and headed for the school cafeteria in the South Wing. It was still lunch period, and she wanted to talk to any of the softball players she could find.

Minutes later she stood in the doorway of the crowded lunchroom, scanning the tables for a familiar face.

Over by the window, Nancy saw Kit Washuta and Cindy Destino sitting with two other girls from the softball team, Debi Hander and Trisha Lewis. She made her way over to them.

"Great game yesterday," she said. "Mind if I join you?"

Kit gestured to an empty chair. "If you can stomach the food, you're welcome."

Nancy laughed. "I think I'll pass on lunch. I've got vivid memories of eating a lot of stuff here that no one could identify."

Cindy poked at a sticky orange mass on her plate. "It was probably this. I mean, I have no idea of what it is, but I'm sure it was left over from last year."

"You're obviously not here for the gourmet food." Debi Hander grinned. "What's up?"

"I'm still trying to figure out who's responsible for the break-in," Nancy said.

Shooting the others a questioning glance, Debi

52

said to Nancy, "Did you know that Louisa Esposito was seen hanging around the school on Saturday and yesterday, too, before the game?"

"So what?" Kit broke in. "Louisa likes to work out when Coach Marks isn't here. Being cut from the team was really rough on her. I think that if you're looking for suspects, you ought to look at Coach Marks."

"Why would she demoralize the team by taking the mascot?" Nancy asked.

"To fire us up against Red Rocks, maybe," Kit suggested. "All during practice she kept complaining that we didn't have enough spirit and we'd never win. She wanted to make us mad."

"I can't believe she'd do that," Cindy said at once. "Coach is tough, but she's not a thief."

"No, but she is vindictive," said Tyra Walker, overhearing these last words as she joined the table. "Guess what I just saw? The coach marching Louisa into Dr. Ryan's office."

"Now what?" Kit groaned.

"Coach Marks says Louisa was responsible for stealing the mascot," Tyra reported. "She's demanding that Louisa be suspended!"

6

Intruder in the Night

"I think I'd better go see Dr. Ryan right away," Nancy said, jumping to her feet.

"It won't do any good," Kit told her. "Teachers always stick together. If Coach Marks wants Louisa suspended, she's out."

"Not if I can help it," Nancy promised.

The bell rang as Nancy left the cafeteria, and she had to push through crowds of students on the narrow stairways. It seemed to take forever before she was standing in front of the closed door to the principal's office.

Nancy knocked loudly on the principal's door. Behind her, she heard Mrs. Leiberman, the school secretary, say, "Nancy! You can't go in there. Dr. Ryan is in the middle of an important meeting."

Nancy, however, kept knocking, and in a moment the door was flung open by Coach Marks. "What is it?" she snapped.

"I have to talk to Dr. Ryan," Nancy said, glancing into the office. She saw Louisa sitting in one of the big leather chairs, her eyes bright with tears.

"Nancy, I'm afraid I have to ask you to come back later," the principal said.

"Later will be too late," Nancy said, stepping into the office. She faced the coach squarely. "I heard that you want to suspend Louisa for the break-ins."

"This is none of your business—" Coach Marks began.

"I'm investigating the break-ins. It *is* my business," Nancy argued. "And I don't think it's fair to suspend Louisa without proof."

"She was trying to sabotage the team," Coach Marks insisted.

"Then why did I find the mascot's jersey in the Red Rocks locker room?" Nancy asked.

An expression of disbelief crossed the coach's face. "You what?" she gasped.

"Nancy found the mascot's jersey in the Red Rocks locker room during the game," Dr. Ryan explained. "I was just about to tell you that. I don't think it's conclusive proof that the Red Rocks girls are responsible, though.

"But by the same token," the principal went on, "unless you can give me concrete proof that

Louisa was the culprit, I can't suspend her. Louisa, did you break into the trophy case and take the items that were inside it?"

"No," Louisa said, her voice shaking. "I would never do anything like that."

"She's lying—" Coach Marks began.

"Don't call me a liar!" the girl shot back. "You just can't deal with anyone you can't control! You don't want a team, you want a bunch of robots!"

"Do you see how disrespectful she is?" the coach demanded of the principal. "Are you going to tolerate this kind of behavior?"

"Louisa—" Dr. Ryan said.

But it was too late. Louisa bolted from the principal's office, tears streaming from her eyes.

Nancy started after her at once. She followed the girl out of the office and into the still-crowded corridors. Louisa was darting through the halls, somehow managing to pick her way through the crowds.

It figures I'd have to chase an athlete, Nancy thought wryly as she struggled to keep up. She saw Louisa's trim figure disappear up ahead, heading for the South Wing. Nancy followed, but when she reached the doors leading out into the parking lot from the South Wing, there was no sign of Louisa Esposito. The girl had vanished.

Well, that was useless, Nancy thought. For a moment she stood undecided about what her next move would be. She knew she'd have to question Coach Marks sooner or later, but it might be wise to wait until the coach was in a better mood. In the meantime she ought to inspect the gym more thoroughly. She'd have to get permission from the principal, though.

A few minutes later Nancy was back in the main office. "I'm sorry," Mrs. Leiberman said as Nancy came in, "but Dr. Ryan's on the phone right now."

"I was just wondering about the objects that were stolen," Nancy said. "Have the police—"

"Officer Nomura was already here," the school secretary said. "She and Dr. Ryan said everything was returned in perfect shape."

Nancy smiled at the secretary's ability to answer her question even before it was asked. Her father had once joked that it was Mrs. Leiberman who really ran the school. Without her, he said, nothing at River Heights High would get done.

The door to the principal's office suddenly opened, and Dr. Ryan came out, looking composed as always. "Nancy," she said, "were you able to talk to Louisa?"

"No," Nancy said. "I never caught up with her. But I was wondering if I could borrow the keys to—" She stopped as she saw the principal's attention shift to someone who'd just entered the office.

Nancy turned and saw the art teacher behind her. "Just came in to drop off that order for art

57

supplies," Mr. Calabrese told the principal. Dr. Ryan nodded at him.

Then Nancy saw Mr. Berger, the custodian, walk into the office. He handed an envelope to Mrs. Leiberman, saying something about an invoice for the boiler parts.

"You were saying, Nancy?" the principal asked.

"I'd like to examine the stolen objects that were returned," Nancy explained.

"Of course," the principal said. "Mrs. Leiberman, can you give her the key?"

"Actually," Nancy said, "I was wondering if I could examine them later. Dr. Ryan, would it be all right if I stayed in the school overnight? I'd like to do some research after school hours. After all, that's when the break-in occurred."

"I don't like the idea of you being here all by yourself," the principal said doubtfully.

"I'm sure I can get Bess Marvin to stay with me," Nancy offered quickly. "We'll bring sleeping bags and camp out."

The principal hesitated. "Very well," she said at last. "On the condition that you don't do this alone."

At about six o'clock that evening, Bess met Nancy in the high school parking lot. Nancy took her sleeping bag out of her car. Bess took a sleeping bag and bulging backpack from hers.

"What have you got in there?" Nancy asked, nodding toward the pack.

"The essentials," Bess replied matter-of-factly. "Sandwiches, cookies, a thermos of soup, a bag of marshmallows, and my blow-dryer."

"Your blow-dryer?" Nancy asked in amazement.

"Of course," Bess said. "I never go anywhere without my blow-dryer. I mean, my hair could frizz out at any moment, so I've got to be prepared."

"I guess so," Nancy said. She couldn't imagine that a blow-dryer would be necessary, but she was glad Bess had brought the food.

Nancy tucked her car keys, wallet, and a flashlight in her fanny pack, and the girls headed for the school entrance.

"So where should we set up camp?" Bess asked.

"I figured we could spend the night in the gym," Nancy answered. "I've asked Dr. Ryan to have it left open for us, and she's given me the key for the trophy cabinet. I also want to do some research in the library."

"Fine with me," Bess said. "But it's going to be weird being all alone in the school."

"I know what you mean," Nancy said as they climbed the marble steps. She pushed a buzzer next to the locked front doors.

Moments later Dr. Ryan opened the door to let

59

them into the empty school. "You're right on time," she said. "I'm the last one here today, and I'm about to head home. You two will be the only ones in the building." She looked at Nancy carefully. "Are you sure you want to do this?"

"Positive," Nancy said.

"Well, then, good luck," the principal said.

Nancy and Bess made their way through the deserted North Wing to the gym, where Nancy headed straight for the trophy case. "It's good to see all this stuff back in place," she said to Bess. The portrait of Dorothy Hunt was once again centered on the back of the case, the mascot's head and jersey on the middle shelf, and the sports trophies added wherever they could fit.

"I bet Gordon McTell was relieved to see his costume returned," Bess said. "It's too bad he couldn't wear it to the last game." Bess's blue eyes suddenly lit up. "That's it!" she cried.

"What's it?" Nancy asked.

"Someone stole the mascot's outfit because they wanted to get back at Gordon McTell," Bess suggested. "And the person took all the other stuff as well, so no one would guess the motive."

"I'm not sure getting back at Gordon was the the motive," Nancy said skeptically. "Somehow I don't think he's a key player in all this. But the second thing you said—that someone might have stolen everything in the case because of one object—that's a real possibility."

60

Nancy took out the key Mrs. Leiberman had given her and opened the display case's glass door. First she took out the familiar portrait of Dorothy Hunt. The gray-haired woman had been painted wearing her favorite blue and white school polo shirt. She was smiling at her viewers, her sharp blue eyes filled with confidence. Nancy carefully examined the portrait and its polished wood frame.

"What are you looking for?" Bess asked.

"Just checking to make sure it hasn't been tampered with," Nancy said. She grinned at her friend. "You know—no stolen rubies rattling around in a hollowed-out frame, that sort of thing."

Next she examined the large papier-mâché wildcat's head. "Doesn't seem to be anything hidden here either," she said, running her fingers along the inside of the hollow skull. She smiled at the cat's fierce expression, its white fangs bared in a snarl. "It's kind of cute. I can see why Gordon got so attached."

One by one, Nancy examined the trophies and then the mascot's jersey. "As far as I can tell, Officer Nomura's right," she said. "Everything was returned undamaged. Let's check out the library and get some background information."

Nancy returned the items to the case. Then she and Bess made their way down a series of darkened hallways to the library, which was also on the North Wing's ground floor. It, too, had been left open at Nancy's request.

Nancy went over to the two shelves that held the collection of River Heights High yearbooks.

"Where do we start?" Bess asked.

"With Miss Hunt's portrait," Nancy answered. She did a few mental calculations, then went on, "Dr. Ryan said Mr. Calabrese painted the portrait when he was in art school. I don't know how old he is, but I'd guess he was in art school sometime in the late sixties. Let's start with 1967."

Bess got down the 1967 yearbook, and the two friends began to thumb through the slightly yellowed pages.

"This is great!" Bess said enthusiastically. "Look at these dresses and hairstyles. They're all coming back into fashion!"

"They almost don't look old," Nancy agreed, taking in the girls' short skirts and the boys' long hair.

"Hmmm . . . 1968 looks a lot like 1967," Bess said, taking up the next yearbook.

Nancy was soon paging through the 1969 yearbook. "No painting of Miss Hunt so far," she said. "But look, here's Mr. Calabrese when he was a senior here—he was on the track team. I almost didn't recognize him without his beard."

"Look at those bony knees!" Bess said with a giggle. "Let's find his senior picture." Bess soon located Mr. Calabrese's photo and read the caption beneath it aloud. "Most likely to be the next great painter of the century."

"I wonder if Mr. Calabrese ever thinks about that," Nancy said. "He's certainly a terrific teacher, but he's never made it big as an artist. Let's see," she went on. "If he was a senior here in '69 and entered the art academy the next year, then Miss Hunt's portrait would have been painted sometime between 1970 and 1974."

Nancy finally found what she was looking for in the 1971 yearbook—a three-page spread honoring Dorothy Hunt. One full page was given to a full-color reproduction of the portrait. There was also an article about it. " 'The painter, William Calabrese, an R.H.H.S. grad, is now in his second year at the art academy,' " Nancy read aloud.

"What about the mascot's costume?" Bess asked. "It wouldn't date back to the seventies."

"No, we should probably start looking about ten years back," Nancy said.

The mascot's head, they soon found, had been sculpted five years earlier by an art student. A "before" photograph showed the girl covering a large chicken-wire shape with strips of newspaper soaked in paste. An "after" photo showed the mascot cheering the team at a football game.

While Nancy studied the photos for clues, Bess took down a more recent yearbook. "I want to see if I can find a picture of Zach Griffith, that totally cute jock who graduated two years ahead of us," she said.

Nancy groaned. "Let's not spend all night looking at old yearbooks. Besides, I'm getting hungry."

"Please," Bess wheedled. "I'll go get some snacks for us."

Nancy sighed. "Okay," she agreed. Bess trotted out of the library, and Nancy leafed through the yearbook for Zach's graduating class. He had been a heartbreaker, she remembered with a smile. Just about every girl in her class had had a crush on him.

She turned to the sports section, where Zach appeared on nearly every page. Caught up in the photos, Nancy barely heard the click of the light switch. One second she was looking at Zach's handsome face, the next the library was plunged in darkness.

Every muscle in Nancy's body tensed. The room was pitch-black, the school silent—except for the sound of footsteps coming toward her.

Relax, Nancy told herself, it's just Bess. She must have hit a light switch accidentally.

And then Nancy remembered something— Bess was wearing sneakers. But whoever was walking toward the library clearly had on leather-soled shoes.

7

Danger Wears a Mask

Instinctively Nancy crouched low to the floor. While she and Bess had been reading the old yearbooks, afternoon had faded to evening. Now it was dark outside. The only source of light in the library was a dim yellow reflection of a streetlight, shining through one of the tall windows.

Nancy waited for her eyes to adjust to the darkness. The footsteps were coming closer. Where's Bess? Nancy wondered. Had she met whoever was walking toward the library? Nancy hoped her friend was safe.

Staying low to the floor and moving as silently as she could, Nancy began to make her way out of the darkened library.

The footsteps came closer, falling with a heavy, watchful tread. It was a man, Nancy decided, or else a very large woman.

Nancy's heart began to pound as the door to the library was pulled open. Quickly she slid behind the book-return desk, hoping that the tall counter would keep her hidden.

The intruder was moving more quietly now. Though Nancy couldn't see beyond the desk, she had the definite feeling that the person was searching for her.

Unable to suppress her curiosity, Nancy peered around the corner of the desk. The intruder was standing just a few feet from her in a shadowed corner of the room.

Nancy couldn't make out any facial features, but from the body's outline she knew that the intruder was a man, his figure lean and menacing.

Instinct told her that he was searching for her. Nancy willed herself to breathe deeply and stay still. She knew that the slightest movement would give away her location. This was a test of nerves, and she was determined not to lose.

The man stood quietly, listening, and then his head suddenly jerked toward her. Nancy sat motionless, trying to slow the rapid beating of her own heart.

At last the man began to move again, and Nancy again risked peering out from behind the desk. Still in the dark, he was going through the room systematically, pushing aside tables and chairs and bookshelves.

Nancy's breath caught as he passed directly in

front of the window lit by the streetlight. Now she understood why she couldn't make out his features. A black cloth mask covered his face.

The man continued to search the library. I need a distraction, Nancy thought, something that will keep him busy long enough for me to get out of here and find Bess.

Nancy reached up to the shelves of the return desk. Careful not to make noise, she began to feel around for something she could use. Her hand closed on a stack of paper, some pens, a rubber stamp, and a heavy metal container that felt like a can of rubber cement.

I could throw this at him, Nancy thought. But can I trust my aim in the dark?

Instead, crawling to the edge of the return desk, she sent the can of glue spinning across the linoleum-tiled library floor.

The man whirled to see what had caused the sound. Nancy took off immediately. Without a backward glance, she sprinted for the library door.

Yanking it open, she raced toward the gym, hoping to find Bess. No matter who was chasing her, she couldn't leave the school without knowing that her friend was safe.

In the distance behind her, Nancy heard a man's voice curse as he jerked open the library door. She heard his footsteps pounding down the hallway behind her.

Now what? Nancy wondered frantically. She pulled at a classroom door, only to find it locked. She pulled at a second door with the same result.

Nancy knew that the North Wing formed a rectangle around an outdoor courtyard. Leaping to that side of the hallway, she tried one of the doors leading to the courtyard. It, too, was locked.

They're *all* locked, Nancy realized with a sinking feeling. The only doors that are open are the ones that I asked Dr. Ryan to leave that way—the library and the gym.

Nancy kept running. The intruder's footsteps grew louder, bouncing off the rows of metal lockers, echoing through the empty halls. He was gaining on her!

Nancy skidded on the slick linoleum floor as she rounded a corner in the dark hallway.

Suddenly the sound of the man's footsteps stopped as another sound filled the empty halls—a high-pitched motor of some sort.

Nancy stopped, too. What *is* that? she wondered, listening keenly.

Then, in the darkness ahead of her, a familiar voice whispered, "Nan!"

"Bess?" Nancy breathed.

"This way," Bess hissed, just barely audible over the motor's whine. "There's an open window at the end of the hall."

That must be how he got in, Nancy thought.

But this wasn't the time to ask questions. She followed her friend in a hurried dash to the window. After hoisting themselves swiftly through the window, they lowered themselves to the ground.

Nancy kept running. She was the first to reach her car, with Bess close behind her. Her hands shook as she took her keys from her fanny pack and opened the car. It was only when she and Bess were safely inside with the car doors locked that she felt herself begin to relax.

"First stop, a phone booth to call the police," Nancy decided.

"All our stuff is still in the gym," Bess said in a worried tone.

"We'll get it tomorrow," Nancy replied as she pulled out of the parking lot. "And not *all* of our stuff is in the gym. That was your blow-dryer in the hallway making that noise, wasn't it?"

Bess gave a soft laugh. "When I went back to the gym to get our snack, I couldn't figure out what I wanted to eat, so I decided to bring my whole pack with me," she explained. "I was down the hall from the library when the lights suddenly went out. And then I saw this figure sneaking toward the library!

"I knew you'd need a distraction," Bess went on. "So I got out my dryer, and I felt along the wall till I found an outlet. Then I plugged it in and waited. I just kept praying that he'd only turned off the light switch—that he hadn't cut the power completely," she added.

"And when I ran out of the library with him in pursuit, you turned it on," Nancy finished.

Bess nodded. "Then I went the other way around the hall till I met you. Thank goodness, the North Wing has a rectangular floor plan!"

"Thanks for the rescue, Bess," Nancy said as she pulled up at the curb next to a pay phone.

"No problem," Bess answered, but she sounded upset.

"Something's wrong," Nancy said. "What is it?"

Bess gave her a mournful look. "My blow-dryer's still in the school. How am I going to do my hair tomorrow morning?"

Nearly an hour later, Nancy and Bess were sitting in a River Heights police station, filling in a written report on the intruder.

Officer Nomura entered the station as Nancy was signing her name to her account of the evening's events.

"I just got back from the high school," the police officer said, taking off her hat. "We called Dr. Ryan, of course, and she asked if you'd drop by the school in the morning."

"Of course," Nancy said. "Did you find the intruder?"

"No," Officer Nomura answered. "He was

70

gone by the time we answered the call, and he didn't leave tracks. There were no prints, no sign of a break-in. He must have gotten in through the first-floor window that Bess found open."

"I wonder who left the window open," Bess said.

Nancy gave a wry smile. "It probably won't do me any good, but I'll ask Mr. Berger about it." She looked at the police officer curiously. "Was anything missing?"

Officer Nomura shook her head. "The library was as you said you left it. The yearbooks were lying open on the table. Some of the tables and bookshelves were pushed aside. Otherwise, nothing was touched."

"That's because he was looking for me. I'm almost certain of that," Nancy said.

"Maybe he thought *you* were an intruder," Nomura suggested. "A teacher or a custodian might have felt it was his responsibility to check out who was in the library after hours."

"Then why didn't he turn on the lights? Why did he come in through the window?" Nancy pointed out.

"That's a good point," Nomura agreed. "But did anyone know you were staying in the school overnight, besides Bess and Dr. Ryan?"

Nancy thought a second. "Mrs. Leiberman. Also, both Mr. Calabrese and Mr. Berger were in the office when we were talking about me spending the night. But I don't know if they heard anything."

Officer Nomura made a note of this. "The art teacher and the custodian," she said. "What kind of motive would either one of them have to stalk you that way?"

Nancy shrugged. "None that I know of." The art teacher had always been friendly and nice. But she couldn't help remembering how belligerent Mr. Berger had been when she'd questioned him earlier that day.

"I do know that this doesn't seem like either Louisa's work or Carla Richmond's," Nancy went on. "It was definitely a man in there."

Officer Nomura tapped a pencil against the edge of the desk. "What if Louisa or Carla has a boyfriend?"

"Louisa does have a boyfriend," Nancy said, "but I can't believe Steve Jackson would pull something like this."

"Definitely not," Bess added. "He just got a scholarship to Stanford University. He wouldn't risk it by breaking and entering."

Officer Nomura didn't look convinced. "I hope you're right. I tried talking to both Louisa and Carla the day after the game, but neither one was very talkative." She gestured toward her badge. "This uniform is sometimes more hindrance than help. People freeze up when I walk into a room."

The police officer's dark eyes grew thoughtful. "Actually, you might do better with them than I did," she suggested. "Carla seems like a pretty tough character, but Louisa might speak to you."

"I'll try," Nancy said, "and I'll let you know what I find."

Officer Nomura reached into a paper bag she'd set down on the desk and pulled out Bess's blow-dryer. "Is this yours, Nancy?"

Bess grinned. "It's mine, actually. Thanks for rescuing it."

Nancy frowned as a new possibility occurred to her. "What if the window was left open as a ruse?"

"What do you mean?"

"I mean, what if the intruder didn't come in through the window at all?" Nancy explained. "What if he either had keys or, like us, was in the building when it was closed? Maybe he left the window open so we'd think that's how he got in—so we'd think this wasn't an inside job."

"That's entirely possible," said Officer Nomura. "But I still don't have much of a crime here. The things that were stolen were replaced. And aside from some library furniture that was pushed aside, I have no sign of last night's intruder, only the report that you and Bess filed. So I'm afraid I can't give this kind of case a very high priority."

"I understand," Nancy said. "And that's all right. It leaves more for me to do. I like a good puzzle."

Officer Nomura's brow creased with worry. "I don't like puzzles that endanger people's lives. Maybe that guy was just trying to scare you off. But I don't like to think about what might have happened if he'd found you."

"Neither do I," Nancy said with a shiver.

"I'm glad you're on the case," the police officer said. "But be careful, Nancy. Something very strange is going on at River Heights High School. I think the break-in was only the beginning."

8

The Stalker Waits

Nancy woke the next morning, still wondering who had been stalking her in the school library the night before. Now that she was safely out of the situation, the full danger of it hit her.

What if he had had a gun or some other weapon? Had he come in the window, or had he been inside the school all along? Had he been alone, or had there been an accomplice somewhere else in the school building, too?

Carson Drew walked into the kitchen as Nancy pondered these questions over a bowl of cereal. "And what are you up to today?" he asked.

"I've got to go back over to the school," Nancy answered. "Dr. Ryan asked me to drop by."

Mr. Drew frowned. "Nancy, I'm glad you want to help Dr. Ryan, but I don't like the idea of you being stalked by someone."

75

"I don't like it much either," Nancy said in a serious tone. "I promise I'll be careful, Dad."

Her father sighed and turned on the small TV in the kitchen. Nancy winced as Ally Laval's smiling face filled the screen.

"Last night the River Heights police received a report of an intruder at River Heights High School," the reporter began. "Famed amateur detective Nancy Drew and her friend Bess Marvin were investigating the recent break-in at the school when a masked man reportedly chased them through the halls."

"She's making it sound like we met Batman," Nancy groaned.

"No suspects were apprehended," Ally finished cheerfully. "All of the objects stolen in Sunday's break-in have been returned, though Ms. Drew continues to work on the unsolved case. Either there is more to this case than meets the eye, or Nancy Drew doesn't like to admit she's failed."

Carson Drew looked at his daughter with concern. "That's a pretty nasty bit of coverage."

"I can take it," Nancy assured her father. Kissing him goodbye, she went out to her car and once again drove to the high school. As she drove, she wished she could solve the case—and she wished Ally Laval lived in another country.

Nearly an hour later Nancy finished giving Dr.

76

Ryan a detailed account of the events of the previous night. "I was wondering if I could borrow two keys," Nancy said.

The principal's dark eyebrows arched in surprise. "If you're asking to spend another night in the school, the answer is no."

"No, that's not it at all," Nancy assured her. "But I'd like to borrow the key to the school and the key to the gym for about an hour. They may help me find an important clue."

Sighing, the principal asked Mrs. Leiberman to give Nancy the two keys she wanted from the principal's set. Nancy immediately drove to SafeKey, the locksmith's shop on Main Street. A few other stores in town reproduced keys—mostly hardware stores—but SafeKey was known as the most reliable.

Inside the small shop, Nancy handed the locksmith the two school keys. "Could you copy these for me?" she asked.

The locksmith, a small, balding man who wore thick eyeglasses, took the keys from her. "Can't do that," he told her after looking them over.

"Why not?" Nancy asked.

He pointed to the tops of the keys. "These can't be reproduced. First of all, they're not made from your standard blanks. Second of all, they have DND on the top. That means Do Not Duplicate. If I copy them for you, I could lose my license." He gave her a suspicious look. "Why do you want to copy them?"

"I don't," Nancy explained. "These keys are from River Heights High. I'm trying to find out if anyone else might have copied them recently."

The locksmith sat down on the bench behind the counter. "Now that you mention it, about a week and a half ago someone else came in with a set of DND keys. I don't remember if it was these same keys."

"What did he look like?" Nancy asked.

"It wasn't a he. It was a she," the locksmith said. "She looked like a high school kid. A small-boned girl with long, dark hair, kind of delicate features. I think she was wearing some kind of school jersey."

Nancy's heart sank. The description sounded like Louisa Esposito.

"Do you remember anything else about her?"

"Yeah," the locksmith said. "She looked nervous. Real nervous."

Once again Nancy was standing in Dr. Ryan's office. "I came to return the keys," she said. "I tried to get them copied in town."

"Why didn't you tell me that's what you wanted to do?" the principal asked. "I could have saved you a trip. These keys can't be copied."

"That's what the locksmith told me," Nancy said. "He also said that someone came into his shop about a week and a half ago, asking to have another set of DND keys copied." She hesitated, then added, "It was a girl matching Louisa's description."

The principal got up from her chair and went to the window. "That doesn't necessarily mean it was Louisa, or that she had the school keys."

"No," Nancy said, "but I need to prove that. Would you mind if I questioned Louisa now?"

Dr. Ryan went to her phone and picked it up. "Mrs. Leiberman," she said, "could you look up Louisa Esposito's schedule and tell me which class she's in now?" There was a pause, then the principal said, "She's absent today? Thank you."

Dr. Ryan put down the receiver and looked at Nancy. "Louisa's not in school today," she said.

"I wonder if that's a coincidence," Nancy mused. "Could you tell me if Steve Jackson's here today?"

The principal looked surprised at the request but did as Nancy asked. After a quick call to Mrs. Leiberman, she answered, "Steve is here. He's in Mr. McNeil's honors English class."

"Then if it's all right, I'd like to ask him a few questions," Nancy said.

Dr. Ryan nodded. "I'll call Mr. McNeil now and tell him you're on your way. It's Room 201."

Nancy went to the second floor and knocked on the door of Mr. McNeil's classroom. Seconds later Steve Jackson joined her in the hallway.

"Hey, Drew," he teased. "I knew that if I waited long enough, one day you'd come after me."

Nancy stared into his gray eyes, wondering if his joking contained a double message. Did he know he was a suspect in the case? "Steve," she said, "can you tell me where you were last night between six and nine?"

Steve's teasing expression faded. "Yeah, I was working my job at Magpie's Pizza from five-thirty until closing time, at ten."

"And what about Louisa?" Nancy asked. "Do you know where she was last night?"

Steve looked surprised. "Louisa? She was home when I called her on my break, at about eight. She said she wasn't feeling very well." Steve's eyes narrowed. "Coach Marks put you up to this, didn't she? She's had it in for Louisa from the start."

Nancy sighed. "Coach Marks hasn't put me up to anything, but maybe it's time I asked her a few questions. Thanks for your help, Steve."

"Any time," he said, returning to class.

Nancy started toward the gym when a familiar voice called out, "Hello, Nancy!"

"Mr. Calabrese," Nancy said, surprised. She hadn't realized she was right by the art room.

80

The tall, bearded teacher, dressed in a baggy blue sweater and paint-specked brown cords, stood smiling, leaning against the doorway of his room. "That was some game on Sunday!" he said.

"It was pretty amazing," Nancy agreed. "I can't believe we finally beat Red Rocks."

"So what are you doing here today?" Mr. Calabrese asked. "Did the softball victory get you so excited about River Heights High that you decided to come back?"

Just then their conversation was interrupted by a girl dressed in overalls and a T-shirt. "Excuse me, Mr. C.," she said, "but could I come work in the art room during lunch? I need to finish my collage."

"On one condition, Laura," the teacher replied. "That you bring me a decent cup of coffee, preferably with a whole-wheat doughnut."

"No problem." The girl grinned. She turned to go and then turned back. "Oh yeah, Louisa called me last night. She said she was sick and asked if you would put the clay vase she made in the pottery kiln this morning."

"Will do," Mr. Calabrese promised as Laura dashed off down the hall. The art teacher shrugged at Nancy. "You can't get a decent cup of coffee in this school. I have to bribe my students to bring it in from the local doughnut shop."

"Is that Louisa Esposito who's out sick?" Nancy asked.

"Yes," the art teacher replied. "She's taking my pottery class, fourth period."

Nancy felt relieved. It sounded as if Louisa really was sick today, not just avoiding school for some reason.

"Speaking of art," Nancy said, "I guess you heard the painting of Dorothy Hunt was returned."

Mr. Calabrese nodded. "Along with everything else in the trophy case."

"Dr. Ryan told me you painted it when you were in the art academy," Nancy said. "How did you ever get a commission like that when you were still in school?"

"Sheer talent," the art teacher joked. "Mr. Curry, who was the principal here then, was extremely impressed with my work when I was a student. The truth is, Mr. Curry didn't know anything about art. But when the school board voted to honor Dorothy with a portrait, Mr. Curry told them he knew an artist who could do it—me. And even though I was only twenty, I got the commission."

"What was Dorothy Hunt like?" Nancy asked him.

"She was a great lady," Calabrese recalled warmly. "And a great coach. She really cared about the kids on her teams. She wasn't into this discipline thing, like some coaches are." He gave Nancy a knowing look.

He means Coach Marks, Nancy realized.

Just then a student stuck his head out of the classroom and asked Mr. Calabrese for some help on his artwork. Waving goodbye to Nancy, the teacher went back inside, and Nancy continued on to the gym.

The gym was empty, but Nancy found Coach Marks sitting in her office, leafing through equipment catalogs. The coach's office hadn't changed at all in the last year, Nancy noted. She took in the familiar surroundings: the photos on the wall of Coach Marks and her teams, the big metal first-aid box, hockey sticks leaning up against the corner, a jar of liniment on her desk, and a River Heights banner hung on the back wall above a small wood hoop holding a number of keys.

"What can I do for you, Nancy?" the coach asked in a friendly tone.

"I want to talk to you about Louisa Esposito," Nancy began.

"All right," the coach said, leaning back in her wooden desk chair. She pointed to the chair at the side of the desk. "Have a seat, and then tell me—how well do you know Louisa?"

"Not very well," Nancy admitted, sitting down. "I've really only spoken to her once."

"Then you have no idea of how difficult she's been," the coach said. "You've been in my classes, Nancy. You know that I'm fair, but I expect everyone to do what's best for the team, not for themselves. Louisa has tremendous talent, but she refuses to be a team player."

"That doesn't make her responsible for the break-ins," Nancy pointed out.

"No," the coach agreed. "But I've been teaching for fifteen years, and if there's one thing I know, it's the girls I coach. Louisa simply couldn't accept team discipline. She was furious when I cut her, and she wanted revenge. She wanted us to lose Sunday's game."

Nancy took a deep breath, knowing that what she was about to say might anger the coach. "It seems to me that you've already convicted Louisa in your own mind."

Coach Marks shrugged. "This is one case that's very clear," she said.

Nancy stood up. "I don't mean any disrespect," she told her former teacher. "But I've had some experience as a detective, and I know you need evidence—real physical evidence—before you can make an accusation like that."

The coach looked as if she was about to respond, but at that moment the bell rang, signaling the end of the period. Immediately after the bell stopped ringing, an announcement came through on the school's public-address system:

"Will Nancy Drew please see Custodian Harvey Berger in his office?"

"How does he know I'm here today?" Nancy asked aloud. After her last interview with Berger, she didn't think he'd want to see her again. Maybe Dr. Ryan told him I'm here, she thought.

The coach stood up. "I'm afraid I have a class coming in now," she said. "I'll see you later, Nancy."

Curious, Nancy left the gym and made her way down to the basement. Again she was greeted with the warm, musty smell as she entered the narrow corridors of the lower level. And again she was aware of how quiet and deserted it seemed.

The basement hallways were dimly lit and the walls in need of fresh paint. Nancy followed the main hallway to an even narrower passage, one that led past the boiler room to the custodian's office.

She was almost halfway there when she felt an odd sensation—the hairs along the back of her neck were prickling. Nancy whirled around. Behind her the hallway was empty.

My instincts must be on overdrive, she thought wryly. There's no one here.

She took two more steps and stopped. She turned and again gazed down the empty hallway. Something was wrong, but she didn't know what.

It's your imagination, she told herself as she started toward the office again.

Then she gasped as a gloved hand grabbed her

roughly from behind. It clamped down across her mouth. Another hand covered her eyes.

Though Nancy struggled furiously, she felt herself being pushed down the hall. She heard a door opening, and then she was shoved hard.

Nancy fell to the floor and glanced up quickly. The last sliver of light disappeared as the door slammed shut. She was alone, trapped in a small, pitch-black space.

On the other side of the door, a key turned, locking her in.

9

Hungry for Revenge

Nancy reached out in the small dark space. Immediately her hand hit something metallic. It fell to the floor with a clang, and the thick smell of turpentine spilled out, filling the air.

Choking, Nancy tried to stand up. A smooth rounded wood stick cracked across her shins.

It's a broom, she realized. I'm in some sort of storage closet.

Her eyes were watering from the turpentine, and she was beginning to feel dizzy. She knew she had to get out the closet soon, before she lost consciousness.

Nancy tried the doorknob. The door was still locked. She groped around the knob, hoping to find a thumb-piece to unlock it from the inside. Like many older storage closets, however, this one seemed to lock from the outside only.

Reaching into her purse, Nancy pulled a credit card from her wallet. Now that her eyes had adjusted, she could just see a crack of light through the edge of the closet door. Halfway up, it was blocked by the dark shape of the lock's bolt. She inserted the credit card, trying to push open the bolt.

She jammed the plastic card against the bolt. Nothing moved. She tried again, coughing so hard that her entire body shook.

On her third try she managed to wedge the card between the bolt and the doorjamb. As she tilted the card, the bolt slid back. Again Nancy turned the door handle, and this time it opened.

She stumbled into the hallway, squinting against the glare of the bare lightbulbs. She took in deep lungfuls of air, waiting for her coughing and choking to stop.

"Hey!" said a rough voice. "What's all the commotion down here?"

Nancy looked up to see the tall figure of Mr. Berger coming toward her.

"You ought to know," she said angrily.

"What?" he asked. He took a sniff of the air. "Did you spill turpentine?"

Nancy pointed to the closet. "I was pushed into that storage closet, where the turpentine spilled all over me. After *you* had me paged, asking me to come down to your office."

"I don't know what you're talking about," the janitor said angrily.

"You had me paged," Nancy repeated.

The gray-haired man shook his head. "I've got better things to do with my time. I don't like snotty-nosed kids down here, asking questions."

Nancy ignored his rudeness. "Just after the bell rang, there was an announcement asking Nancy Drew to please come to Mr. Berger's office," she insisted patiently.

"Well, if there was, I didn't have anything to do with it," the custodian snapped.

"Didn't you hear it?" Nancy asked.

Mr. Berger pointed to a small Walkman hanging from his belt. "When I work, I'm always plugged in. Can't hear a thing except my music, and I like it that way."

"Fine," Nancy said. "I'll just go up to the office and ask them who was responsible for the announcement."

"You do that," Mr. Berger called after her. "And stay out of the broom closet!"

Minutes later, Nancy was in the office, waiting for Mrs. Leiberman to finish a phone call.

"Nancy," Mrs. Leiberman said, wrinkling her nose as she hung up the phone. "Oof! Did you get mixed up with some turpentine?"

"I guess you could say that," Nancy answered, smiling in spite of herself. "Mrs. Leiberman, did you page me just after the bell rang?"

"Yes, I did," the secretary said. She frowned at Nancy. "Do you want a change of clothing? I'm sure we have something in the Lost and Found that would fit you."

"That's all right. The smell of turpentine makes me feel artistic," Nancy joked. "But could you tell me why you paged me and asked me to go to Mr. Berger's office?"

The school secretary held up a rectangular wire basket that sat on the edge of her desk. "Teachers and other staff members leave announcements in here. I check the basket at the end of every period and read whatever's in there."

"So you didn't see who put the announcement in?" Nancy asked.

Mrs. Leiberman shook her head. "No, dear. I was in Dr. Ryan's office, doing some filing. When I came out, the message was in my basket."

Nancy took a deep breath. "Do you still have the message?" she asked.

"I put it in my recycling bin after I read it," Mrs. Leiberman told her. She pointed to a plastic rectangular container. "Look in there."

"Thanks, Mrs. Leiberman," Nancy said.

It didn't take Nancy long to find the slip of paper. Handwritten in neat, rounded script, the message was exactly what she remembered hearing: Will Nancy Drew please see Custodian Harvey Berger in his office?

"Mr. Berger said he never asked for me to be paged," Nancy told the secretary. "Would you mind if I compared the handwriting on this note with Mr. Berger's writing?''

Mrs. Leiberman frowned. "I'll see if I can find a sample of his writing. Maybe there's something in his file—something I can show you that won't violate his privacy, of course."

A few minutes later, Nancy sat comparing the note against an envelope from Mr. Berger's file. The envelope bore an address written in the custodian's handwriting, a tight, narrow back-slant. It was clear, just from those three lines, that the two handwriting samples were not the same.

"I think Mr. Berger was telling the truth," Nancy said. "Someone else had this announcement made." She gestured toward the announcement slip. "Do you mind if I take this with me?"

"It's all yours," the secretary assured her.

Well, Nancy thought as she left the school building, I'm not much closer to solving the case. Whoever came after me, it wasn't Mr. Berger— not this time, at least. But at least I know that someone *is* trying to stop me. And if someone's taking the trouble to stop me, it's because there's something major to hide.

Nancy started across the school parking lot toward her blue Mustang. She slowed as she saw a Jeep pull into the lot, a short distance from where she was parked.

Five teenagers—three girls and two boys— piled out. All of them were tall and athletic-looking. And all wore Red Rocks letter jackets.

Nancy recognized one of the five: Carla Richmond. Why would Carla and her friends show up at River Heights? Nancy wondered. She had a feeling they could mean only trouble.

"Hi," Nancy called out, going up to them as if they were friends. "What are you guys doing here in the middle of the school day?"

One of the boys shot Carla an uneasy glance. Looking defiant, Carla answered, "It's our lunch period. We're allowed to leave the school then."

"It's a long drive over from Red Rocks," Nancy pointed out.

"Well, we figured we'd come visit our favorite rivals," Carla sneered. "We thought maybe we'd have a little game of catch."

With that, Carla turned back to the Jeep and took out five softball mitts and handed them around to her friends. Nancy walked on to her own car, trying to look unconcerned.

Out of the corner of her eye, Nancy saw Carla take out a softball and a wooden bat. She rested the bat against the Jeep, and she and the others began a casual game of catch, right there in the parking lot.

Equally casually, Nancy started to unlock her car. She didn't trust Carla or her friends, but she thought it best to leave the school, then call Dr. Ryan from a pay phone. The principal would want to know about the visitors from Red Rocks.

Nancy had just opened her car door when she

heard Carla's voice behind her. "So what are *you* doing here, Miss Detective?"

Nancy turned toward her calmly, noting that Carla now held the bat in her hand. "I'm still trying to figure out who took our mascot before the game," Nancy answered.

"You mean you're still trying to frame me," Carla snapped accusingly. "I suppose now you're going to search the Jeep like you searched the locker room the other day."

"I never tried to frame you," Nancy told her.

"Then why did your principal call our principal and tell him I stole the jersey?" Carla demanded, advancing on Nancy. "She threatened to have us thrown out of the athletic conference!"

"Easy, Carla," said the taller of the two boys who was with her.

"Last time I saw you, I warned you," Carla said to Nancy angrily. "I didn't expect to see you here today, but now I realize you're the one I have to settle a score with. It's because of you that I was cited for 'unsportsmanlike' behavior."

"More likely it's because you deliberately hit Tyra with the ball," Nancy retorted.

She saw a flash of rage cross Carla's face. Carla swung the bat high, aiming at the headlights of Nancy's Mustang.

"I wouldn't move if I were you," Carla spat out at her. "You do, and I'll destroy this car."

93

10

A Cryptic Clue

Nancy watched in disbelief as Carla Richmond swung the wooden bat hard at her headlights. She's crazy, Nancy thought. She's really going to destroy my car.

But the bat never connected. At the very last second, the shorter of the two boys grabbed Carla by the shoulders and pulled her away from the car. "Carla, stop it," he said in a calm but firm voice. "You're only going to make things worse. It's not worth getting yourself in more trouble for her."

"Yeah," said one of the girls. "Let's just get out of here. We have to get back for classes, anyway."

Carla struggled for a moment against the boy's hold and then calmed down. "Fine," she said, "we'll leave. But I'm still going to get you,

94

Drew!" she promised. "You're going to be sorry you ever went near Red Rocks High!"

"Carla Richmond actually threatened you?" Bess asked the next afternoon as she and Nancy sat in their favorite booth in Yogurt Heaven. Nancy had wanted to talk things over with Bess earlier, but Bess had been staying overnight at a friend's house in a neighboring town.

Nancy took a spoonful of the frozen chocolate yogurt in front of her. "Carla Richmond likes making threats," she told Bess. "The question is, has she actually done anything worse than that?"

"She certainly has!" Bess said indignantly. "She nearly took Tyra out of the game. She almost creamed your car with a baseball bat. And she stole the mascot's jersey."

"We don't know about that last one for sure," Nancy said.

Bess dug into her low-calorie yogurt "sundae" —vanilla yogurt covered with blueberries and strawberries. "Carla's probably the one who wrote that awful announcement you told me about and pushed you into the broom closet."

"I don't think so," Nancy said. "She and her friends from Red Rocks drove into the parking lot just as I was coming out of the school. Besides, they had no way of knowing I would be at River Heights yesterday."

Bess didn't look convinced. "When you told Officer Nomura that the intruder in the library was a man, she said either Louisa or Carla could have enlisted a boyfriend to help. Do you think either of those guys with Carla yesterday was her accomplice?"

"I don't think so," Nancy said. "Both those guys were trying to calm Carla down. They didn't want to get into trouble. And Louisa's boyfriend, Steve, has an alibi. I checked it out last night—when we were in the library, he was definitely working at Magpie's Pizza."

Bess finished the last of her sundae. "So who do you think pushed you into the broom closet?"

"I'd like to think it was Mr. Berger," Nancy answered, "mostly because he's such a grouch. But I have proof that he wasn't the one who wrote the announcement to get me into the basement. Someone else is trying to get me off the case, and I'm becoming convinced that it's someone who works at River Heights High."

"Well, I still think we need to talk to Louisa," Bess said.

Nancy smiled at her friend. "That's exactly what I was thinking. But when I called Mrs. Leiberman an hour ago, she said Louisa was absent again today."

"Then we'll have to visit her at her house," Bess said. "We ought to be able to find her address in the phone book."

The two girls went to the restaurant's pay phone and consulted the telephone directory. There was only one Esposito listed. "Do you want me to call her first?" Bess asked.

"No," Nancy replied. "I think it's best if we surprise her. There are a lot of things I want to know about Louisa Esposito, including whether or not she's really home sick."

Bess looked slightly regretful. "I was sort of hoping we'd have time for another yogurt sundae. I know they're helping me lose weight." Bess was always trying to lose five pounds. "Don't I look thinner to you?"

Nancy smiled at her friend. "I think you always look great," she said honestly. "If you want another sundae, why don't you get one to go?"

As Bess went to the counter to get her second sundae, Nancy left a tip on the table and headed out of the booth. She stopped as a well-dressed woman with dark, glossy hair entered the restaurant.

"We meet again!" said Ally Laval, flashing her TV-perfect smile.

"I guess so," Nancy said without much enthusiasm.

"You should be happy to see me," the reporter said. "I know that the stolen items were returned to the school, and I know you still don't have a clue as to who's responsible. And I just might have the tip you need to break the case."

97

"Really? What is it?" Nancy said sweetly.

Ally shook her head. "That would be too easy. After all, you're the hotshot detective."

Nancy glanced impatiently toward the counter, where Bess was still waiting in line.

"If you don't mind me asking, why *is* this case taking so long to solve?" the reporter went on.

Nancy shut her eyes, hoping that when she opened them again, Ally would be gone. When she opened them, Ally was still standing there— but so was Bess, her sundae in her hand. "Nan, I'm sorry to interrupt," she said in a rushed voice, "but I'm running late for my appointment with the veterinarian. We really have to go."

"Right," Nancy said, picking up her cue. "Sorry, Ally."

Without giving Ally a chance to respond, Nancy and Bess hurried out of the restaurant.

"Do you want a clue?" Ally called out just as they reached the door.

Nancy turned, unable to resist anything that might help her solve the case.

"If you want to know where to find the information I have, check the rabbit with the disk," the reporter said smugly.

"The rabbit with the disk?" Nancy echoed.

"And burp the zebra with the potato," Bess muttered. "It makes as much sense."

Nancy elbowed Bess to be quiet. "Thanks a lot," she called back to Ally.

Inside the car Nancy glanced at her friend and grinned. "The veterinarian?" she asked. "Bess, you don't even have a pet!"

"I know that," Bess said. "But we needed an excuse to get away from Ally. I was going to say 'vegetarian' because I was thinking about a new diet I might try, but somehow 'veterinarian' was what came out."

"Well, I'm glad. It was inspired," Nancy said. "Let's hope we're equally inspired when we talk to Louisa."

Louisa Esposito lived in a large apartment complex in the northern section of River Heights. Nancy and Bess crossed a grass-covered court-yard, and then peered up at the four towering cement and glass buildings above them.

Nancy glanced down at the address she'd copied from the phone book. "The Espositos are in D tower."

"Over there," Bess said, pointing to the far-thest building.

The two friends entered and then took an elevator to the eleventh floor. The Espositos' apartment was at the end of the hall.

Bess rang the bell. Nancy heard footsteps in-side, then the door opened a crack. Nancy got a glimpse of worn tan carpeting and overstuffed furniture.

"Bess!" Louisa said, opening the door fully.

She was wearing an old plaid bathrobe over a thin cotton nightgown. "What are you doing here?"

"I came to see you," Bess answered. "Are you all right?"

Louisa nodded, but she looked unhappy. "Come in," she said.

"Louisa, you remember Nancy Drew," Bess said.

Louisa gave Nancy a wan smile. "Thanks for trying to stop Coach Marks the other day."

"What finally happened?" Nancy asked.

Louisa let them in and then sank down on a gray corduroy couch. "I wound up in the bathroom, crying. Tyra came in and found me there and persuaded me to go see Dr. Ryan again. Dr. Ryan said I'm not suspended—yet."

"If you weren't suspended, then why are you home?" Bess asked. "Are you sick?"

Louisa answered with a hollow laugh. "Beats me. I feel lousy every morning when I wake up. My mother said if I'm not better tomorrow, I have to go to the doctor. She thinks I'm just depressed about what's going on at school."

"But Dr. Ryan is on your side," Bess said.

"No," Louisa said, "Dr. Ryan refuses to take sides. I think she's just waiting until she has proof that I was responsible for the break-in."

"Were you?" Nancy asked gently.

"No," Louisa said. "For the hundredth time, no, I did not break into the trophy case and take

100

that stuff. Hey, it's Marks I'm mad at, not the team or the school. If I'd wanted revenge, I would have done something to *her*." Louisa shut her eyes and leaned back against the couch.

"Someone told me you said you'd do anything to ruin her," Nancy said.

When Louisa spoke, her voice sounded weary. "I know I said that, but I was just angry." She groaned. "I can't even believe this whole mess! If Marks gets me suspended, my chances for a college scholarship are shot. All I did was miss three practices, and she's about to wreck my entire life."

"Louisa," Nancy said, "did you bring a set of the school keys to SafeKey to be copied?"

"What?" Louisa opened her eyes and ran a hand through her long, dark hair. "Where would I get a set of school keys?"

Bess looked confused. "I thought school keys were the kind of keys that couldn't be copied."

"They are," Nancy assured her.

Suddenly Louisa sat up. "Oh," she said.

"Oh, what?" Nancy asked alertly.

Louisa's dark eyes were wide with fright. "I can't tell you," she said.

"Louisa, we're trying to help you," Nancy said.

"I had nothing to do with the break-in," Louisa said. "You just have to trust me on this."

Frustrated, Nancy decided to try another tack. "Was it someone you know? A friend, maybe?"

Louisa stood abruptly, looking apologetic. "I haven't even offered you two anything to drink. Let me see what's in the fridge."

"Louisa—" Nancy said. But Louisa was already on her way to the kitchen.

"She's hiding something," Nancy said quietly.

Bess nodded unhappily. "But I still believe she's telling the truth about the break-in."

"So do I," Nancy said. "At least, I want to." Then she noticed a spiral-bound notebook lying on the living room coffee table. Louisa's name was written on the front cover.

Nancy picked up the notebook and idly began to flip through it. Then she stopped. She realized that the handwriting looked familiar.

Not wanting to be right this time, she opened her purse and took out the announcement she'd taken from Mrs. Leiberman's wastebasket.

"Oh, Bess," Nancy said softly. "The handwriting looks exactly the same!"

11

An Ugly Warning

Nancy swiftly tore a page from Louisa's notebook and folded it into her purse. She hoped it would be a while before Louisa noticed that the page was missing.

As she waited for Louisa to return from the kitchen, Nancy debated whether or not to show her the announcement she'd found in Mrs. Leiberman's recycling bin.

I have to show it to Louisa, Nancy thought. I have to give her a chance to explain herself.

But she never got the chance. At that moment the door to the apartment opened and Louisa's mother walked in, grocery bags in her arms.

"Hi, Mrs. Esposito," Bess said quickly. "I'm Bess Marvin. I heard Louisa's been sick, so I dropped by to see if she's okay. This is my friend Nancy Drew."

103

Mrs. Esposito smiled hello and set the bags down on the dining room table. Louisa returned from the kitchen, holding a tray with a pitcher of orange juice and three glasses.

"Louisa, you shouldn't have friends over when you're sick," her mother scolded gently. "You ought to be in bed, resting."

"I think your mom's right," Nancy said. "We ought to go. I hope you feel better soon."

"I'll call you, Louisa," Bess promised as they left the apartment.

The two friends were back in Nancy's car before they spoke. "That wasn't very helpful, was it?" Bess asked as they drove away from the apartment complex.

Nancy shrugged. "It's like every other phase of this case. I get a little information, but not enough to form any sort of pattern."

She counted off the recent encounters on her fingers. "Louisa says she didn't break into the trophy case—and I believe her—but her handwriting matches the announcement that called me to Mr. Berger's office. Carla Richmond says she's innocent and then tries to destroy my car with a baseball bat. Mr. Berger says he hasn't done anything, but somehow I wind up locked in a broom closet!

"Meanwhile, Coach Marks clearly has it in for Louisa," Nancy added, sighing. "If I can't find a way to explain Louisa's handwriting matching the writing on this note, I just may have to take the coach's accusations seriously."

"Oh, Nancy, you can't mean that!" protested Bess.

Nancy gestured helplessly. "Everyone's suspicious and I don't have a single lead."

"There's always Ally Laval's helpful clue," Bess reminded her in a sarcastic tone.

"Right," Nancy said grimly. " 'Check the rabbit with the disk.' Whatever that means."

"It'd be just like Ally to give you a false clue," Bess said. "What has she got against you, anyway?"

Nancy rolled her eyes. "I think she's just obnoxious to everyone."

But long after Nancy had dropped Bess off, Ally's clue was echoing in Nancy's mind: "Check the rabbit with the disk. Check the rabbit with the disk." Did "disk" mean a computer disk or a compact disc or a spinal disk, or could it be something like a Frisbee? And who or what was "the rabbit"?

Unlike Bess, Nancy was fairly sure there was a real clue buried in Ally's nonsense. She just hoped she could uncover it before Louisa was suspended.

That evening Nancy did what she often did when she was stuck on a case: she talked it over with her father. They sat in Carson Drew's cozy study and discussed the case over a pitcher of iced tea. Nancy loved her father's study, with its book-lined shelves, deep leather chairs, and leaded glass windows looking out into the sycamore trees.

Nancy began by laying out the facts, right up through the visit with Louisa. "So you see why I'm stuck," she finished.

"I do indeed," her father said. "There are a number of very puzzling points. You don't think Red Rocks was responsible for the break-in, do you?"

"Not really," Nancy said. "For one thing, it was done with too much finesse. Carla's style is to come out swinging with a bat. There's nothing subtle about that girl."

"So then," her father said, "how did the mascot's jersey wind up in her gym bag?"

"I've been trying to figure that one out for days," Nancy admitted.

Mr. Drew pressed his fingertips together, a habit of his when trying to work out difficult problems. "Let's say someone planted the jersey in Carla's bag. And if we go with your theory that it was an inside job, then it was someone from River Heights High. Who had the opportunity to get into the Red Rocks locker room?"

"Just about anyone who was at the game," Nancy answered. "It was open, and during the course of the game nearly everyone left the stands at one point or another. I know I did, and so did Ms. Stamos and Mr. Calabrese."

"That's not terribly conclusive," her father said. "Let's try another line of reasoning."

Nancy smiled. Sometimes her father sounded as if he were cross-examining her. But it was discussions like these with her dad that had taught Nancy how to examine a case, how to look at every aspect until something broke it open.

"You said both Mr. Berger and Mr. Calabrese heard you tell Dr. Ryan that you wanted to stay in the school overnight," Carson Drew went on. "And both are tall men who could have been the stalker. Could either of them also have been responsible for the theft?"

"Mr. Berger, easily," Nancy replied. "He's got keys to the gym. Mr. Calabrese, not so easily—either he would have had to break in and hide inside, or get someone to copy the keys to the gym for him." Nancy's blue eyes suddenly lit with excitement. "Maybe *that's* what Louisa didn't want to tell me!" she said.

Carson Drew raised his eyebrows, and Nancy filled in the details. "I asked her about copying the keys, and her reaction was really strange—as if she *had* brought in keys to copy but had no idea that they were keys for the school. And I know she's one of Mr. Calabrese's students."

"Also far from conclusive, but maybe we're getting somewhere," Mr. Drew said cautiously.

"There's still one thing that bothers me. You said that the stolen objects had sentimental value only, that they weren't really worth much."

"That's true," Nancy agreed.

"But where there's theft, there's usually money involved," her father said. "Even though we can't see how anyone could get money from this theft, you still might look at the financial status of your suspects. Check out a group of people—Coach Marks, Mr. Berger, Mr. Calabrese, Ms. Stamos, even Dr. Ryan—and see if any of them is having obvious financial difficulties."

"How would I do that?" Nancy asked.

Carson Drew raised one eyebrow. "You could ask your old father to help you out."

Nancy laughed. "I'll take any help I can get. And while you're at it, how about some help on a bizarre clue that Ally Laval gave me: 'Check the rabbit with the disk?"

"That's it?" he asked, baffled.

Nancy nodded.

"Sounds to me as if Ms. Laval would have you checking every computer disk in town," he said.

"But for what?" Nancy asked. "For something connected with a rabbit? There hasn't been anything remotely rabbitlike in this whole case."

"No, there hasn't," her father agreed. He finished his iced tea and glanced at his watch. "I think we need a break. The weekly movie classic on TV just started. Care to join me?"

"Might as well," Nancy said.

Nancy and her father settled down in front of the living room TV. The movie was an old James Stewart film about a man who insists that his best friend is a six-foot-tall invisible rabbit named Harvey.

"That's it!" Nancy said, sitting bolt upright on the couch.

"What is?" her father asked.

"The rabbit part of the clue," she said excitedly. "The rabbit's name is Harvey. This is a famous movie—I'm sure Ally Laval must have seen it. 'The rabbit' is a substitute for the name Harvey."

"You've lost me," Carson Drew murmured.

Nancy tried to keep the excitement out of her voice, but she failed. "Don't you see—Harvey is Mr. Berger's first name!"

"So?" her father asked, with a bemused expression on his face.

"So . . . I don't know," Nancy admitted. "Except that Ally Laval thinks I should be checking out Harvey Berger."

That night Nancy found it difficult to sleep. She lay in bed, unable to stop thinking about the case or about the rest of Ally Laval's baffling clue. Now that she'd guessed what "rabbit" meant, what did the word "disk" mean?

She was just drifting into a dream when a loud crash brought her awake again.

Sitting up in bed, Nancy switched on her

bedside lamp. She blinked in astonishment at what she saw.

Her bedroom window was shattered. Among the shards of broken glass, a large rock lay on the carpet. Attached to the rock was a note, printed in letters cut and pasted from a magazine. Nancy read the note aloud:

"'Back off, Nancy Drew, or you'll regret it!'"

12

Something to Hide

As Nancy stared at the threatening note, she heard her father calling through the bedroom door, "Nan, are you all right?"

Nancy opened her door. "I'm fine, Dad," she said. "But the window's not in very good shape."

Carson Drew took in the situation at once. "I'll call the police," he said in a tight voice.

Twenty minutes later Officer Nomura and a police photographer were in Nancy's room, photographing the window and the note. Dressed in her bathrobe, Nancy sat cross-legged on her bed, filling out yet another police report. She updated Officer Nomura on what had happened that day.

"I'm going to take the rock and note for evidence," the police officer said when the photographer was done. "And, Nancy," she added, "I'd like you to take this warning seriously."

"You want me to back off the case?" Nancy asked in disbelief.

"It might be a good idea to lie low for a while," Officer Nomura replied.

"I can't do that," Nancy said. "I think Louisa Esposito's being framed. I'm not sure who's doing it or how, but I can't drop this case until I know for sure."

Nancy woke late the next morning, still exhausted. Sleepily she made her way downstairs and found a note from Hannah on the kitchen table: Nancy—I have a dentist appointment this morning. Would you stay around until the people who are going to fix the window show up?— Hannah."

Nancy poured some cereal into a bowl, wishing she didn't have to stay home. She didn't exactly know where she should start that day, but she needed to be out working on the case. Well, she decided, I might as well read the morning paper. It's been days since I've had a chance to do that.

Nancy reached for the copy of the *River Heights Morning Record* that her father had left on the table. Her hand froze in midair. Her eyes lingered on the masthead, as if seeing the paper's name for the first time.

"The *Record*," she said aloud. "A record can also be a disk. 'Check the rabbit with the disk' means 'check Harvey with the *Record*'!" she said, finally understanding Ally Laval's mysterious clue. Nancy knew now what her next step was—a trip to the *Record* office. The past issues on file must hold some information on Harvey Berger.

Just then the phone rang, and Nancy picked it up to find her father on the line. "If you stop by my office at lunchtime," he said, "I might have some information for you."

"Thanks, Dad," Nancy said. "I'll be there."

The phone rang again almost as soon as she hung up. This time it was Bess.

"Morning, Nan," said Bess. "I was just thinking. Yesterday, Louisa acted so funny when you asked her about copying the keys. Maybe she *had* tried to have those keys copied, but she didn't realize what keys they were."

"That's how it seemed to me," Nancy agreed.

"Well," Bess went on, "I was just wondering— if they were the keys to the gym, where do you think she got them?"

Nancy thought for a moment, and then remembered something she'd seen in Coach Marks's office the day before. "Coach Marks keeps that wooden key ring hanging right on her office wall," she said. "Louisa—or someone else— could have just 'borrowed' it if the coach were suddenly called out of her office."

"But wouldn't Coach Marks have reported her key ring missing?" Bess asked.

"Maybe," Nancy said, "but not if she found it

again a short time later. Everyone misplaces keys at one time or another."

"So you think that someone got the coach's keys and had Louisa make copies?" Bess asked.

"It's possible," Nancy said. "And whoever that person is, I think he or she knows I'm closing in on them." Then Nancy told Bess about the warning note she'd received the night before.

"This is getting serious," Bess said, worried. "Is there something I can do to help?"

"Actually, there is," Nancy answered. "I'm stuck at home until the window repair people show up. Do you think you could do a little research for me at the *Record* office? I need you to go through some back issues of the paper."

"No problem," Bess said. "What do you need?"

"See if you can find anything about any of our suspects at River Heights High—particularly Harvey Berger. But while you're there, see if there's anything on anyone else connected to the case: Coach Marks, Carla Richmond, Louisa, Mr. Calabrese, even Ms. Stamos."

"Done," Bess said. "I'll be in touch later today. Try to take it easy this morning, okay?"

"I'll try," Nancy said, but she knew that she wouldn't relax until the case was solved.

It seemed forever before the repairman from the window company showed up. He took his time, putting a new sheet of glass in the window of Nancy's room. As he handed Nancy his bill, Nancy saw Bess's car pull up in the drive.

"Who was that gorgeous guy who just came out of your house?" Bess asked as she walked in.

"The window repairman," Nancy said, amused.

Bess wriggled her eyebrows. "Really? He's extremely cute." She glanced at the bill on the table. "And he makes good money."

"My dad's going to love that one." Nancy grinned. She glanced at her watch. "Speaking of my dad, I've got to go to his office. But first, did you have any luck at the *Record*?"

Bess handed Nancy a thin manila envelope. "I photocopied a few articles for you," she said, sitting down at the kitchen table. "Before coming to River Heights High, Mr. Berger was the custodian at Shoreham Elementary. Guess why he got fired."

Nancy scanned the newspaper story. "He was accused of stealing school supplies. Though it looks like the case never went to court."

Bess helped herself to orange juice. "No, he resigned first. And he claimed he was innocent."

Just as he claims he's innocent now, Nancy thought. "And what's this?" she asked, picking up a copy of an article about the school board.

"Look who appeared before the board this fall," Bess said.

"Mr. Calabrese and Coach Marks," Nancy

read. "They were arguing over funds. Mr. Calabrese said the money should go to an arts program, and Coach Marks wanted it for girls' athletics."

"And here's the follow-up," Bess said, handing Nancy another column. "The money went to girls' athletics."

Nancy sat at the kitchen table. "So Mr. Calabrese and Coach Marks have been opponents. And Mr. Berger's been accused, if not convicted, of stealing from another school."

"There's one more," Bess said, her blue eyes sparkling. "This picture was taken at last year's faculty picnic."

Nancy stared at the photograph of a group of River Heights faculty, dressed in shorts and T-shirts. "There's Mr. Li," she said. The boys' gym teacher had been caught leaping for a Frisbee. "And there's Mr. Calabrese," she said, spotting the art teacher sitting on a picnic blanket in the corner. "Who's that sitting next to him?"

"Ms. Stamos!" Bess said triumphantly. "They must have known each other before she transferred to River Heights. Look at the way his arm is draped around her shoulder."

"But what does it prove?" Nancy asked.

Bess shrugged. "I don't know. Maybe that they've been plotting something together?"

116

Nancy gave Bess a wry grin. "I believe my father would call that evidence not terribly conclusive. But this other story—the one about Berger—is interesting. One question, though: If he is a thief, why would he want to steal a school mascot?"

Nancy slipped the articles back inside the envelope. "Thanks, Bess. I'm going to check in at my dad's office now. He said he'd have some information for me, too."

"Sit down, Nan," Carson Drew said, ushering Nancy into his office.

"Were you able to get financial information on our suspects?" Nancy asked.

"Well, not bank records, no," her father said. "But one of my associates handles lots of real estate transactions. She tells me that three months ago Mr. Calabrese tried to buy a house."

"What happened?" Nancy asked.

"He couldn't find a bank that would give him a mortgage," Mr. Drew answered. "Now, Mr. Calabrese has been teaching at River Heights for years. Normally, someone with a stable job like that has no trouble getting a mortgage unless—"

"He's having real financial difficulties," Nancy finished.

Her father nodded. "I wasn't able to get any

information on your other suspects, but we can reasonably say that, as of three months ago, William Calabrese needed money."

"William Calabrese," Nancy echoed. "As an art teacher, he's the one person who should be totally unconnected to the theft of a sports mascot, and yet his name keeps coming up." Nancy began to tick off items on one hand. "He painted the picture of Dorothy Hunt in the first place. He was at the game when the jersey was planted in Carla's gym bag. And he overheard my telling Dr. Ryan I was going to spend the night in the school. Louisa is one of his regular students. And now I learn he's in some kind of financial trouble."

"Those five facts may or may not be linked," Carson Drew said warily. "You can't afford to jump to conclusions here."

"I know that, Dad," Nancy said. "But my instinct tells me they aren't all coincidental. I'm going to see what else I can find out about his connection with Louisa Esposito."

"What can I do for you, Nancy?" Mrs. Leiberman asked a short time later, as Nancy walked into the high school office.

"Is Louisa Esposito in school today?" Nancy asked.

Mrs. Leiberman checked the attendance record for Louisa's homeroom. "Yes, she is."

118

"May I check her schedule?" Nancy asked. "And last year's as well?"

The secretary pushed her glasses up on her nose. "Dr. Ryan said to give you whatever help you need. Let me see what I can find." The older woman typed something into her computer and a second later hit a print command. "Here you go," she said, handing Nancy the two schedules a few moments later.

Nancy skimmed them quickly and saw what she'd suspected. For the past two years, Louisa had taken an art class with Mr. Calabrese every semester. This term she had pottery class during fourth period—which was right then, Nancy realized, glancing at her watch. Maybe she could catch Louisa between classes and ask her a few questions.

"Thanks for your help, Mrs. Leiberman," she said as she headed out of the office.

Nancy hurried down the hall, wishing the art room wasn't upstairs on the opposite side of the North Wing. She came to an abrupt halt as she nearly collided with Gordon McTell, who was carrying a large cardboard box.

"Careful!" he said indignantly. "I left class early just so I could get this to my car safely, without having to go through the hordes."

"Sorry," Nancy said. "What is it?" Curious, she peered into the open box. Inside was a ceramic sculpture of a small cougar, sitting on its haunches. The wildcat's fur was striped in the River Heights High blue and white.

"I made it," Gordon said, "in pottery class."

"You take art, too?"

Gordon rolled his eyes. "Lots of people do."

"Are you in Louisa Esposito's class?" Nancy asked.

"Yes," Gordon said impatiently.

"Tell me," Nancy said, "is Louisa serious about art?"

"As serious as she is about sports," Gordon said. "If she doesn't get a sports scholarship, she'll get one for art. The first time she missed one of Coach Marks's softball practices, she was finishing up an art project after school."

Gordon leaned closer to Nancy, his eyes gleaming with the delight of a born gossip. "I think the real reason Marks is so ticked off at her is because she knows Louisa's part of the Calabrese Club and softball isn't the only important thing in her life."

"The Calabrese Club?" Nancy repeated.

"Yeah," Gordon said, "that's what they call the kids who hang out in the art room and do favors for Mr. C. Louisa's one of Mr. Calabrese's favorites. She—"

An ear-splitting alarm suddenly filled the hallway.

"Fire drill!" Gordon shouted. He sprinted

toward the parking lot, leaving Nancy standing in a hall that was rapidly filling with students.

Terrific, Nancy thought. As the alarm continued to shriek, students poured into the corridor, all heading for the entrances. Nancy had no choice but to join the flow of students heading out of the school.

The school emptied quickly. Outside, teachers gathered in groups and students mingled, enjoying their unexpected break from classes on the balmy late-spring day.

Looking around, Nancy saw no sign of Louisa or Mr. Calabrese. But she did see Dr. Ryan, talking to Ms. Stamos and looking extremely upset.

As Nancy made her way toward the principal, two fire engines, their sirens blasting, suddenly barreled across the parking lot.

Her senses alert, Nancy backed up to scan the school building. There was no sign of smoke or flames, but she knew that fire trucks didn't turn out for mere drills. Had a fire started somewhere in the building?

Two police cars careened into the parking lot, and Nancy knew that something was seriously wrong.

She reached the principal just as the fire chief got out of the first engine. He signaled to his fire fighters, who immediately began to move students away from the building. Other fire fighters, followed by four police officers, rushed toward the school.

"Dr. Ryan," Nancy said. "What's going on?"

The principal turned to her, her face lined with worry. "This isn't a fire drill, Nancy. River Heights High just received a bomb threat."

13

The Case Is Closed!

The students hadn't been told about the bomb
threat but the crowd's mood changed. A tense
silence fell as the fire fighters and police officers
carefully steered everyone away from the building. Fear hung thick in the air.

Nancy wondered what was behind the bomb
threat. Could it possibly be related to the case?
Had the threat come from the same person who'd
sent a rock smashing through her bedroom window?

Forty minutes later, the police and fire fighters
emerged from the building.

"No sign of any bomb," a police officer reported to Dr. Ryan. "But we'd like to go over the
building more thoroughly. It would probably be a
good idea if you dismiss school for the day."

"Of course," the principal said, her composure

returning. The fire chief handed her his bullhorn, and she made the announcement to the assembled students. A halfhearted cheer arose as the kids began to leave the school grounds for the day.

"Dr. Ryan," Nancy said, tagging along after the principal. "How did the threat come in? Did you get a phone call?"

"No, Mrs. Leiberman found a note in her announcements basket," the principal replied, turning around. She still held the note in her hand, and she held it out to Nancy.

Nancy's blue eyes widened as she took in the now familiar script. It looked identical to the note that had sent her to the custodian's office—and identical to Louisa's handwriting.

"We'll need to take that to the station with us," one of the police officers said. Dr. Ryan gave him the note.

"The handwriting on that looks identical to the writing on that announcement request that was made yesterday," Nancy said. She didn't mention Louisa's notebook. She wasn't ready to implicate Louisa until she was completely sure of the facts.

"What announcement?" the police officer asked.

Nancy described what had happened, as she had to Officer Nomura the night before.

The officer gave a low whistle. "You've got someone very sick at work here."

"I'm aware of that," Dr. Ryan said tensely. "And I'm going to start minimizing our risks. It's possible that Nancy's investigation has been annoying whoever is behind this. I'm sorry, Nancy, but as of this moment, the case is closed."

Nancy felt as if someone had just knocked the wind out of her. "What do you mean?"

"I mean that I cannot afford to have you or my students endangered by this investigation. The stolen objects were returned unharmed. As far as I'm concerned, this case is officially closed."

"Don't you see?" Nancy said. "That's exactly what whoever is behind this wants!"

"Nancy," the principal said patiently. "I'm responsible for the safety of my students. I can't risk their safety just so that you can solve a puzzle."

Nancy took a deep breath, wondering how to persuade the principal. "Dr. Ryan, this isn't about me wanting to solve a puzzle," she said. "This is about someone dangerous being loose in River Heights High. Someone has almost attacked me twice, and someone threw a rock through my window last night. Now someone has threatened to blow up the school. This person must be caught."

But Dr. Ryan refused to budge. "If that's true, I'm sure the police can handle it. Go home, Nancy," the principal went on, more gently. "I appreciate all the help you've given us, but it's out of your hands now."

Nancy knew Dr. Ryan well enough to know she wouldn't change her mind, especially with all these other people looking on. Now was not the time to argue.

Feeling discouraged, Nancy made her way through the crowds to her car. Nancy opened her car door, then shielded her eyes as a bright light flashed into them.

"The lighting around her face is fine," a young man said.

"What—" Nancy began. She caught herself as she saw Ally Laval, dressed in a mauve raw-silk suit, standing behind the man who'd just done the lighting test. Beside Ally stood another man with a heavy TV camera on his shoulder.

Oh, no, Nancy thought to herself.

"Just a few questions, Nancy," Ally said. She signaled to the cameraman and began speaking in her professional voice. "This is Ally Laval at River Heights High School, where a bomb threat was received this afternoon. I'm here with Nancy Drew, a young detective who has an impressive reputation for cracking tough cases."

Nancy winced inwardly. She wished she could just get in her car and drive off without looking as if she were running away.

"Nancy, you've been working on the break-in that took place at River Heights High this past weekend," Ally rattled on. "Tell us, please, was today's bomb threat related to the theft?"

Nancy said the only neutral thing she could think of. "No comment."

"No comment?" Ally echoed. "Nancy, the public has a right to know if you're investigating in one of our high schools. Or are you trying to withhold information from us?"

Nancy summoned all her courage and spoke directly into the mike. "I'm sorry," she said, "but at this point I have no comment." Then, without giving Ally a chance to respond, she got into the car and drove off.

"You up for the local news?" Carson Drew asked Nancy later that evening. He and Nancy and Hannah had just finished dinner. Nancy hadn't told either her father or Hannah how badly things had gone that day.

"I think I may turn in early," Nancy replied, yawning.

"Oh, come on, Nan," her father said in a teasing voice. "Don't you want to know what's happening in River Heights?"

Not really, Nancy thought. I already know, and I don't like it.

Mr. Drew picked up his copy of the evening paper and strode into the family room. He switched on the TV.

I could just go upstairs and go to bed, Nancy

thought, but then I'd only have to discuss things with Dad later.

Nancy settled herself on the couch and watched. The news anchor discussed that day's meeting of the county supervisors, then reported on a three-year-old boy who had taught his pet gerbil to skateboard.

"Isn't that charming?" Hannah said.

"Adorable," Nancy agreed. Maybe the news director had canceled Ally Laval's segment, Nancy began to hope. Surely any news professional could tell that Ally Laval was making too much of the bomb threat incident. . . .

"And in a late-breaking story, River Heights High School was evacuated this afternoon when a note with a bomb threat was found," the anchor said. "We go now to on-the-scene coverage with reporter Ally Laval."

Nancy watched tensely as Ally described the bomb threat and evacuation of the school. "This isn't the first hint of trouble at River Heights High," the reporter continued. "This past weekend several objects were stolen from the school trophy case, and local detective Nancy Drew was called in. Here's an excerpt from our interview with her."

"Interview?" Nancy said scornfully, after the footage with her two "no comment" answers was shown. "That's no excerpt," she told her father and Hannah. "That was the whole conversation."

"Shhh," her father said gently. "There's more."

"After interviewing Ms. Drew, I spoke with Principal Ryan about Ms. Drew's role in the investigation," Ally went on. "I asked her if it was true that Nancy Drew had been slow to solve this case and, as a result, was endangering the student body. What Dr. Ryan told me may come as a surprise to most residents of River Heights— Nancy Drew is officially off the case." Ally beamed a dazzling smile at the camera.

"Nancy has been fired," Ally continued, "and the question we all have to ask ourselves is, Has Nancy Drew's illustrious crime-fighting career finally come to an end?"

14

The Final Piece of the Puzzle

The next morning Nancy woke up early. She'd barely been able to sleep the night before. She wasn't sure which hurt more—Dr. Ryan's taking her off the case or Ally Laval's making it public.

Actually, she told herself, neither of those really mattered. What mattered was that Louisa was still in danger of having her future ruined.

Nancy pulled on a white V-neck sweater and a short denim skirt and went downstairs for breakfast. Her father had already left for his office, and Hannah was out doing errands.

Nancy was pouring herself a glass of orange juice when the phone rang. She picked up the receiver and heard the school secretary's crisp voice. "Nancy, this is Mrs. Leiberman. You have to come down to the high school at once."

"Um—" Nancy hesitated. "I appreciate your calling, Mrs. Leiberman. But that may not be such a good idea. Dr. Ryan fired me from the case."

"I know that!" Mrs. Leiberman snapped. "But the parents and the school board have been pressuring Dr. Ryan to do something fast about the disruptions in the school. So now she's about to suspend Louisa."

"She can't!" Nancy said, alarmed. "Suspending Louisa won't stop whoever's been breaking in and leaving bomb threats."

The secretary gave a weary sigh. "That's why I called you. Now, will you please come down here and talk to Dr. Ryan before she does something we all regret?"

Mrs. Leiberman hung up with a loud click. Nancy stood staring at the phone receiver. Then slowly a smile crossed her face. "You didn't leave me much choice, did you?" she murmured.

"Are you sure about this?" Nancy asked Mrs. Leiberman.

"I'm sure," the secretary said. "Just march right into her office and talk to her."

Nancy had never been afraid of the principal, but still, the idea of marching uninvited into her office was a little daunting.

"Go on," Mrs. Leiberman said. "Remember, Louisa's future may depend on you."

Right, Nancy said silently. Summoning her courage, she knocked on the principal's door.

"Come in!" Dr. Ryan called, but when Nancy walked in, her voice became cool. "Nancy, I thought I made myself clear yesterday."

"You did," Nancy said, "but I've heard—a rumor—that you're about to suspend Louisa."

"My, word does get around," the principal said dryly. "Nancy, I must take action."

"Can't you wait one more day?" Nancy pleaded. "If I can't prove by tomorrow that Louisa's innocent, then you can suspend her and I won't say a word. Just give me twenty-four hours."

Dr. Ryan stood up impatiently. "You're not even working on the case anymore—"

"I thought you believed in the presumption of innocence," Nancy interrupted in a calm, firm voice. "No one has any proof that Louisa is responsible for the break-in. You can't ruin her record just because someone *thinks* she's guilty."

"All right," the principal said reluctantly. "I'll give you until tomorrow morning."

Nancy felt weak with relief. "Thank you," she said.

After leaving the principal's office, Nancy went straight to Bess's house. "I've got one more day to solve this case," she explained to her friend. "I'm going to need your help."

"Fine," Bess said, "but we've got a stop to make first."

"What stop?"

"Maggie Thompson called. Actually, she called you and got your machine, so she decided to try my house. Hannah's painting is ready."

Nancy moaned. "Today is Hannah's birthday! I've been so caught up in this case, I totally forgot. I was going to bake a cake!"

"That's why you need me," Bess said, nudging her gently toward the door. "I never forget to shop. Or eat. Come on, let's stop at the gallery, then we can buy a cake at the bakery. It won't take long."

"It's perfect!" Nancy said, admiring the framed painting of the lilacs. She looked up at Maggie, who was dressed in a dusky blue silk kimono and black silk pants. "How did you ever get the orange nail polish off?"

"Trade secret," Maggie said with a wink. "Nail polish remover."

"Wouldn't that take off the oil paint as well?" Bess asked.

"Not if you're extremely careful." Maggie pulled out a paintbrush that was so tiny, it seemed to be made of three hairs. "I used this. Here, I'll show you."

She reached under the office desk and produced another small oil painting marred by a long streak of bright orange. "Didi and her nail polish struck again before I let her go," Maggie explained with a smile.

Maggie dipped the fine brush in the bottle of nail polish remover. Slowly, with remarkable control, she began to remove the streak of orange. Nancy watched, fascinated, as the polish gradually vanished, revealing the original painting below.

"You have to work carefully," Maggie said, "so that you don't ruin the original painting. Restoring art is an art in its own right. Many Italian frescoes were discovered under layers of dirt or beneath another artist's paint."

"I really appreciate your taking the time to do this," Nancy said. "Hannah will love her painting."

The phone rang then. "Excuse me," Maggie said. "Without Didi, I'm back to answering my own phone."

The gallery owner picked up the phone and listened attentively. Nancy's eyes roamed the shelves in the gallery office and fell on the photo album Maggie had shown them.

To pass the time, Nancy took it down and began to look through it. She stopped at the photograph of Horenstein when he was at the art academy. "Bess," she whispered, "doesn't this guy on the right look familiar?"

"It's Mr. Calabrese!" Bess said. "I didn't recognize him the first time we saw this."

"Neither did I," Nancy murmured.

"Are you sure?" Maggie was asking her caller in a voice filled with cautious excitement. "I can't quote a price over the phone, but I'm very interested in seeing it. Please bring it by."

She hung up the phone and turned to the two friends. "I don't believe it!" she exclaimed. "That man said he has an early Horenstein self-portrait that he'd like to sell through the gallery. He says it dates back to Horenstein's days at the art academy. If that's true, it's worth a fortune!"

Nancy looked thoughtful. "But wouldn't Horenstein's later pictures be better, when he reached his peak as an artist?"

"His later work is technically superior to his college pieces," the gallery owner agreed. "But there's so little of the early work, it's valuable simply because it's so rare."

"Well, good luck with it," Nancy said. "I hope it's the real thing."

"So do I," Maggie said. "Are you two coming to the show on Sunday?"

"We wouldn't miss it," Nancy said. She and Bess left the gallery, this time with Hannah's gift tucked securely under Nancy's arm.

"Now to the bakery," Bess said as Nancy put the Mustang into gear.

Nancy began to head toward Main Street. But halfway there, she suddenly switched directions.

"Nan," Bess said gently, "are you okay? The bakery is in the other direction."

"I know," Nancy said with a smile. "But you know how I've been waiting for the pieces of this case to fit together? Well, I think they finally fell into place! I'll explain on our way to Dr. Ryan's office. I just hope it's not too late."

"Now what?" Dr. Ryan asked as Nancy once again entered her office.

"I think I've figured out who's responsible for the break-in and the bomb scare," Nancy said. "But I'll need your help and Mr. Calabrese's. Do you think you could ask Mr. Calabrese if we could meet him at his house tonight at six?"

"This is a most unusual request," the principal said cautiously.

"I understand that," Nancy said, "but he'll be more willing to help out if you ask him."

"Very well," Dr. Ryan agreed with a sigh.

"One more thing," Nancy said. "Can you bring the bomb threat note?"

"The police have it," the principal replied. "But I'll do what I can to get it back."

At six o'clock that evening, Nancy and Bess pulled up in front of Mr. Calabrese's house. Like the other houses in the neighborhood, it was a small turn-of-the-century bungalow. Painted off-white with pale green trim, it was charming.

As Nancy and Bess parked across the street from the house, a sleek sedan pulled up to the curb behind them. Dr. Ryan got out. "Nancy, Bess," she said, greeting them. "I certainly hope we can resolve this now."

"We will," Nancy promised. "I'm certain of it." But her heart was racing. Things would work out—if her hunch was right. It has to be, Nancy told herself. It just has to be!

Dr. Ryan rang the doorbell. The tall, bearded art teacher opened it with a smile. "Welcome," he said with a slight bow.

He led them into the living room. Nancy was impressed with Mr. Calabrese's simple but lovely home. There wasn't much furniture, but each piece was beautiful. A simple glass vase on top of a low pine table held cascading sprigs of jasmine. Two wooden mission-style chairs stood on each side of a large fireplace. Filmy white curtains framed the tall windows, and each wall was hung with a large oil painting.

"Are those yours?" Nancy asked, gesturing toward the paintings.

"I'm afraid so," Mr. Calabrese joked. "I'm the most affordable artist I know."

"Do you have a studio here?" Nancy asked.

"Just off the living room," Mr. Calabrese answered, and pointed toward it. "It was originally the sun room, so it gets lots of light. It's good for painting."

"Please, Nancy," Dr. Ryan said. "You called us here for a reason. Let's get on with it."

Nancy opened her purse and pulled out the false announcement slip summoning her to the custodian's office, as well as the page she'd torn from Louisa's notebook. She laid them on the dining room table. "Dr. Ryan, do you have the bomb threat?" she asked.

The principal took out that note and laid it beside the other two.

"Mr. Calabrese," Nancy said. "I asked for your help because, of all of us, you've got the sharpest eye for visual detail."

The art teacher folded his arms across his chest and regarded Nancy with amusement. "What exactly do you want me to do?"

"Look at these three handwriting samples," she requested, "and tell me whether or not they were written by the same person."

"Don't they have handwriting experts for this?" the art teacher joked. But he leaned over the table and examined the three samples. "Well," he said, "there are certainly similarities. The rounded hand, the forward slant—"

He was cut off by a loud knocking on the front door. "Excuse me for a moment," he said, stepping away from the dining-room table.

138

Nancy watched as the art teacher opened the front door. Ally Laval pushed her way into the bungalow, followed by a cameraman.

"Wait a minute!" Mr. Calabrese protested. "What's all this about? How dare you invade my home this way!"

"We had a very reliable tip," Ally explained. "Someone told us that the case of the missing mascot was going to be solved here tonight."

Nancy didn't wait around to watch the argument between Mr. Calabrese and Ally Laval. Instead, she headed straight for Mr. Calabrese's art studio.

Nancy's eyes roamed the cluttered studio. A paint-splattered drop cloth covered the floor. Unfinished canvases were propped against two easels. A well-used palette lay on a tall stool, and a fistful of brushes soaked in a glass jar of turpentine on the drawing table.

Nancy found what she was looking for, lying face up on a worktable. She picked it up and carried it triumphantly into the living room.

Mr. Calabrese and Dr. Ryan were both trying to persuade Ally Laval and her cameraman to leave. "Not yet," Nancy said, stopping them. "I think I have the story Ally is looking for."

"What's going on?" Dr. Ryan demanded.

"See for yourself," Nancy said, nodding toward the canvas she was holding.

139

"What's happened to Dorothy?" Bess asked in dismay. For Nancy was holding the portrait of Dorothy Hunt.

But something was wrong with it. Half of the painting seemed to have faded away, and an entirely different portrait was emerging beneath it.

"Dorothy Hunt's was the second portrait to be painted on this canvas," Nancy explained. "Beneath it is an original self-portrait by Burt Horenstein. And it's worth a fortune!"

15

The Perfect Crime

"I don't understand," Ally said, for once looking unsure of herself.

"I'm afraid I do," Dr. Ryan said, her voice stiff with shock.

"Get that camera out of here," Mr. Calabrese ordered Ally. "You've got no legal right to run it in this house. You're trespassing and—"

"He's right, Ally," the cameraman cut in.

"Okay, Herb," Ally said, "turn it off. Now," she went on, "what about this painting?"

"This is the original portrait of Dorothy Hunt," Nancy explained. "Until last weekend it was on exhibit in the River Heights gym. The one that was replaced on Monday was a copy—by the original artist."

She turned to Mr. Calabrese, who was regarding her with an unreadable expression. "Horenstein's portrait was underneath it all along, wasn't it?"

Mr. Calabrese sat down in one of the fireside chairs, seemingly unconcerned by Nancy's discovery. "Burt and I were roommates at the art academy," he began. "One of us became a major artist, and one of us never made it at all." He gave a cynical snort of laughter. "My most valuable canvas was valuable only because it had a Horenstein underneath it."

"I still don't understand how that happened," Ally Laval complained.

Mr. Calabrese smiled briefly. "It's really not complicated," he said. "At the time Mr. Curry gave me the commission to do Dorothy's portrait, I was so broke I couldn't even afford a canvas. So Burt gave me one of his that he no longer needed. We were always helping each other out."

Mr. Calabrese shook his head. "He gave me a canvas with a self-portrait on it that he'd painted for a technique class. Neither of us ever thought it would be worth a fortune."

"But when the Thompson Gallery announced that it was doing a Horenstein retrospective, you realized what that old painting would be worth," Nancy put in.

"I realized it before then—when Burt died and his work immediately tripled in value." Calabrese gave the bitter chuckle of a man poisoned by his own failure and resentment.

"I've thought of staging my own death, you know—just to see if it would make my art go up in value," he went on, gesturing to the paintings on his wall. "Better buy them now, while they're still cheap."

Bess looked perplexed. "So you stole the original painting, with the portrait of Horenstein beneath it, just before the conference game?"

Mr. Calabrese nodded. "I needed the original so I could make a perfect copy of it. It didn't take me long. I painted the duplicate over the weekend, and I returned it early Monday morning with all the other objects. I figured if I stole a number of things, no one would ever guess why the portrait was being stolen."

Nancy nodded. "And when you overheard people speculating about the theft, you framed the Red Rocks students. It was you who planted the mascot's jersey in Carla Richmond's gym bag, wasn't it?"

Mr. Calabrese smiled. "It was too perfect to resist. Everyone was sure Red Rocks was going to sabotage River Heights. I merely planted the evidence and fulfilled their expectations."

"Which you did when you and Ms. Stamos left the bleachers for refreshments," Nancy said.

"Fortunately, Ms. Stamos stopped to talk to her friend," Mr. Calabrese said. "She had nothing to do with this, you know."

"It was all you," Dr. Ryan said, her voice

shaking with anger. "How could you do this to our school? And then try to frame a student—"

"It was the perfect crime," Mr. Calabrese said with a shrug. "It wasn't even a crime—everything stolen was returned, wasn't it? Look at it as more like a loan. I borrowed Dorothy's portrait for a weekend and gave you back exactly what you thought you had all along. What's the problem?"

"The problem," Nancy said, "is that you tried to frame Carla Richmond. And when that didn't work, you tried to frame Louisa Esposito, one of your favorite students! You used her to get you the keys to the gym."

"No one used Louisa to get the keys to the gym," Mr. Calabrese said. "Claudia Marks keeps them right on her wall. I simply slipped into the office when she was busy in the gym and borrowed them."

"But you had Louisa make the copies," Nancy said.

"She found a hardware shop that was glad to do it," Mr. Calabrese agreed.

"And then you forged the two notes in her handwriting," Nancy went on.

Mr. Calabrese looked bored. "That was easy, too. As you said yourself, I have a good eye for visual detail."

"But that wasn't the end of the trouble you caused," Nancy declared. "You were the one who

144

stalked me in the library Monday night. On Tuesday you followed me to the basement and pushed me into the broom closet. You threw the rock through my window Wednesday night and yesterday made that phony bomb threat."

"That many offenses will really add up when you go before a judge." Dr. Ryan sighed. "And it was all to cover up the original theft. Why did you do it in the first place, William?" she asked sadly.

"He needed the money," Nancy said. "He's in financial trouble."

Mr. Calabrese stood up with a sigh. "I think," he said slowly, "that I've had about enough of this."

Then suddenly, as fast as lightning, Calabrese grabbed the painting from Nancy. Pushing past her, he raced for the back of the house.

"Bess, call nine-one-one!" Nancy shouted. Then she tore after the art teacher.

Dashing out the back door after him, Nancy was just in time to see Mr. Calabrese cross the back yard. He slung the painting over the brick wall that enclosed the yard, then vaulted up after it.

Calabrese paused for an instant to glare back at Nancy. Then he disappeared over the wall.

16

On the Run

Calabrese can't go very fast, carrying that canvas, Nancy told herself. But it took her a few moments to scramble over the high wall that the tall art teacher had jumped with ease. When she dropped to the other side, she was in someone else's yard, and Mr. Calabrese was nowhere in sight.

Nancy looked around. The yard was filled with roses—on the walls, on trellises, and on bushes in between. No one could get through this yard, carrying a large canvas, without getting stuck on thorns, Nancy thought. So where was Calabrese? Had he disappeared into thin air?

There was no sign of the art teacher—only a garden, heady with the scent of roses.

And then she saw, behind one of the trellises, an arched wooden door in the wall, slightly ajar.

Annoyed with herself for not seeing it sooner, Nancy hurried through the prickly garden, ignoring dozens of scratches.

The wooden door led to the street. Two blocks ahead, Nancy saw Mr. Calabrese's tall form rounding a corner. She raced after him, forcing a swift pace. I can catch him, she panted to herself. But when she turned the corner, Calabrese was gone.

Nancy slowed, gasping for breath and trying to calm her pounding heart. He's probably hiding somewhere, she reasoned. Or maybe he's hidden the painting, intending to pick it up later. After all, a tall, bearded man running around the streets of River Heights, clutching a large canvas, wasn't exactly inconspicuous.

She debated going back to the house for Bess and decided against it. Calabrese was out here somewhere. She didn't want to risk losing him. Senses alert, Nancy searched the quiet streets.

Twilight was falling. One by one the streetlights came on, but the streets themselves were cloaked in shadows. This part of the chase was always nerve-racking, Nancy knew. There was always the possibility that whoever you were chasing would turn the tables and chase you.

And then, passing a narrow alley between two shops, she heard something. A cat hunting through the garbage, Nancy told herself. But she stopped and peered into the shadows. Was that the corner of a canvas sticking out between those two cardboard boxes?

She started toward it. Suddenly the cartons toppled over. Calabrese, still clutching the Horenstein, was racing away from her.

Nancy took off after him. "Stop!" she cried. Calabrese dashed for the other end of the alley.

And then Nancy saw two police cars pull across the far end of the alley, their sirens screaming and their lights flashing.

Officer Nomura sprang out of the patrol car, reaching for her gun. Calabrese held the painting in front of his chest like a shield. "You'll have to destroy it to get me," he taunted.

"I don't think so," Officer Nomura said. "There are two more officers behind you. Now, put down the painting and put up your hands. The chase is over, Mr. Calabrese."

On Sunday afternoon Nancy helped herself to a quiche puff and a mineral water, then wound her way through the Thompson Gallery, jam-packed with people for the opening of the Horenstein show.

Nancy stood on tiptoe, looking for a familiar face. "There you are!" Bess waved. "I've been looking for you."

"Ditto," Nancy replied. "I can't believe the turnout. Maggie's show seems to be a success."

As Bess scanned the crowd, her blue eyes widened. "Louisa! What are you doing here?"

Louisa sidled over to Nancy and Bess. "I called your house," Louisa said to Nancy, "and your father said you and Bess were here. I wanted to thank you for helping me."

"I'm glad we could," Nancy said. "No one should be framed by a weasel like Mr. Calabrese."

"Do you think they'll convict him?" Louisa asked, looking worried.

"He's pleading guilty," Nancy told her. "He made a full confession to Officer Nomura."

"It's still so hard for me to believe," Louisa said. "For two years he was one of my favorite teachers. I can't believe he faked my handwriting so that everyone would think I was responsible for his crimes."

"Well," Bess said, "you were a convenient scapegoat, especially since Coach Marks seemed determined to run you out of school."

"Have you talked to the coach since Mr. Calabrese's arrest?" Nancy asked curiously.

Louisa smiled. "She called my home last night. It sounded like she was choking on her words, but she apologized for accusing me. She even asked me to play in next week's championship game. Dr. Ryan must have read her the riot act."

"Probably," Nancy agreed.

"The important thing," Louisa said, "is that she won't stand in the way of my getting a scholarship." She looked at Nancy curiously. "What about Mr. Berger? Did you ever find out his story?"

"Officer Nomura did some checking for me," Nancy said. "According to the police files, after Berger left Shoreham Elementary, they found the real thief—the school nurse. But Mr. Berger still mistrusts anyone who starts poking around. That's why he wasn't thrilled when I asked him all those questions."

"So what's Carla Richmond's problem?" Bess wanted to know.

"That's easy," Louisa said. "Everyone in the softball conference knows Carla has a chip on her shoulder. She's always starting fights. Since she's such a strong athlete, her coaches used to let her get away with it. But Coach Marks said that Red Rocks has finally put Carla on probation for next year's sports teams. Once she gets some counseling and shows a marked improvement in attitude, they may let her play again."

"One more question," Bess said. "Nan, why did you take us all out to Calabrese's house to have him compare the handwriting samples?"

"I just needed an excuse to get into his studio," Nancy said. "And I wanted Ms. Ryan and Ally there to see the proof that he had painted over Horenstein's self-portrait."

Bess giggled. "*You* called Ally?"

Nancy smiled. "I knew she'd cause enough commotion to let me get into Calabrese's studio."

Dr. Ryan, looking elegant in a simple black coat dress, joined the girls. "Nancy," she said, "I haven't had a chance yet to congratulate you on solving the case. You and Bess did a wonderful job. And Louisa, I owe you an apology for thinking you might have been our criminal."

"It's okay, Dr. Ryan," Louisa said. "I know you were trying to be fair."

"There you are!" Maggie said, sweeping toward the girls. She wore a long purple silk caftan and strings of silver necklaces. "Nancy, did Hannah like her painting?"

"She loved it," Nancy said.

"Good! There's another painting I'd like to show you—the most valuable one in the show."

Maggie led them to the area of the gallery where the crowds were thickest. People were clustered so tightly that Nancy couldn't even see the wall, let alone any art hanging there. "Excuse us," Maggie called out, shouldering through the throng.

Nancy, Bess, and Louisa followed until they stood at the front of the crowd, a short distance away from a large canvas. On it was an arresting portrait of a young artist, wearing beat-up clothes. There was something haunting about his skeptical expression and his tense, uneasy pose.

Louisa tilted her head to study the painting. "What a fascinating picture!" she breathed. "It was worth all the trouble to bring this back to the public eye."

Beneath the portrait in neat block letters were the words: Burt Horenstein, Early Self-Portrait. On Loan from River Heights High School.

YOU COULD WIN A TRIP
TO THE PARAMOUNT THEME PARK
OF YOUR CHOICE

One First Prize: Trip for three to the Paramount theme park of the winner's choice.

Four Second Prizes: Four Single-Day Admission Tickets to the Paramount Park near you.

Twenty-Five Third Prizes: One Nancy Drew Mysteries Boxed Set and One Hardy Boys Mysteries Boxed Set.

Name_____ Birthdate_____

Address_____

City_____State_____Zip_____

Phone_____

POCKET BOOKS/"Win a Trip to the Paramount Theme Park of Your Choice" SWEEPSTAKES
Official Rules:

1. No Purchase Necessary. Enter by submitting the completed Official Entry Form (no copies allowed) or by sending on a 3" x 5" card your name and address to the Pocket Books/Nancy Drew/Hardy Boys Sweepstakes, Advertising and Promotion Department, 13th Floor, 1230 Avenue of the Americas, NY, NY 10020. Entries must be received by 10/30/94. Not responsible for lost, late or misdirected mail. Enter as often as you wish, but one entry per envelope. Winners will be selected at random from all entries received in a drawing to be held on or about 11/3/94.
2. Prizes: One First Prize: a weekend for three (the winning minor, one parent or legal guardian and one guest) including round-trip coach airfare from the major U.S. airport nearest the winner's residence served by United Airlines or United Express, ground transportation or car rental, meals and three nights in a hotel (one room, triple occupancy), plus three Weekend (Saturday and Sunday) Admission Tickets to the Paramount theme park of the winner's choice (approximate retail value: $3880.26 - $3911.70). Winners must be able to travel during the regularly scheduled 1995 operating season of the Paramount Park chosen (approximately 5/5 - 9/1, 1995). Four Second Prizes: Four Single-Day Admission Tickets to the Paramount Park near you (retail value: $86.84 - $107.80). Twenty-Five Third Prizes: One Nancy Drew Mysteries Boxed Set and One Hardy Boys Mysteries Boxed Set (retail value: $31.92). All dollar amounts are U.S. Dollars.
3. The sweepstakes is open to residents of the U.S. and Canada no older than fourteen as of 10/30/94. Proof of age required to claim prize. Prizes will be awarded to the winner's parent or legal guardian. Void in Puerto Rico and wherever else prohibited by law. Employees of Paramount Communications, Inc., United Airlines and United Express, their suppliers, affiliates, agencies, participating retailers, and their families living in the same household are not eligible. One prize per person or household. Prizes are not transferable and may not be substituted. All prizes will be awarded. The odds of winning a prize depend upon the number of entries received.
4. If a winner is a Canadian resident, then he/she must correctly answer a skill-based question administered by mail. Any litigation respecting the conduct and awarding of a prize in this publicity contest may be submitted to the Regie des Loteries et Courses du Quebec.
5. All federal, state and local taxes are the responsibility of the winners. Winners will be notified by mail. First Prize winner will be required to execute and return an Affidavit of Eligibility and Release within 15 days of notification or an alternate winner will be selected. Winners grant Pocket Books and Paramount Parks the right to use their names, likenesses, and entries for any advertising, promotion and publicity purposes without further compensation to or permission from the entrants, except where prohibited by law. For a list of major prize winners, (available after 11/3/94) send a stamped, self-addressed envelope to Prize Winners, Pocket Books/Nancy Drew/Hardy Boys Sweepstakes, Advertising and Promotion Department, 13th Floor, 1230 Avenue of the Americas, NY, NY 10020.

Nancy Drew Mysteries and The Hardy Boys Mysteries are registered trademarks of Simon & Schuster.

994

YOUR TICKET OUTTAHERE!

SAVE $4 IN 1994 WITH THIS COUPON

PARAMOUNT
CANADA'S
WONDERLAND
TORONTO, ONTARIO
(905) 832-7000

PARAMOUNT'S
CAROWINDS
CHARLOTTE, NC
(800) 888-4386

PARAMOUNT'S
GREAT AMERICA
SANTA CLARA, CA
(408) 988-1776

PARAMOUNT'S
KINGS DOMINION
RICHMOND, VA
(804) 876-5000

PARAMOUNT'S
KINGS ISLAND
CINCINNATI, OH
(800) 288-0808

The Only Place Thrills Are Paramount.™

Now that you're done reading this book, don't just sit there! Get up! Get outta here and into some excellent fun at one of these Paramount Parks! Take on a coaster, take in a show, and most importantly, take off four bucks with this coupon. See ya' there!

Parks are open weekends in the spring and fall and daily during the summer. Operating dates and times, admission prices and policies vary. Call the parks directly for more detailed information.   Got it? Good.

Paramount Parks

A Paramount Communications Company